To My
NADA, NABEEL

The
Hanging
Bird

Monir Metawa

Translated by Chris Ashbolt

Editing, design, typesetting and publishing by UK Book Publishing

www.ukbookpublishing.com

ISBN: 978-1-915338-74-7

For my *Rose*

"I'm done!" she said to herself, feeling her head.

She feels like an electric shock struck her. She doesn't want to give in to despair, but she is afraid that this could be the end.

She has had a turbulent life prior to this defining moment because she is cursed. She has no idea where this curse came from. Has a supreme will dictated that she must endure everything that has happened to her? Was her birth into this world a mistake that she must pay for—though she bears no guilt for it—throughout her life, or the rest of her life, which she now believes is ending, or has already ended without her even being aware of it?

She did not come into the world because of her inclination or free will. Perhaps she would not have existed if the decision had been in her hands. She has not taken a single day off since she realized her own existence. She sees no sign that the days ahead hold any hope for her.

Amal. (Her name means hope.)

This is both her name and her problem.

She has spent the last few years hoping that her one and only wish would come true.

However, nothing happened. The exact opposite occurred. The opposite always happens.

She occasionally considers suicide. In a desperate attempt to realize her hope, she attempted to do away with her life, but it was in vain. She tried again, and when she was rescued, she was disheartened. She couldn't even get rid of her awful life.

Why is it such an awful life? The life of Amal?

This is a long journey and requires patience from anyone who wants to undertake it, follow, station after station and patience from anyone who wants to tell it.

Where have you gone, Amal?

Amal disappeared.

FIRST STAGE

Is there even such a thing as a perfect human?!

Hanging Bird Lane, where things do not come to a halt as though life were about to cease, as though the world had a date with the end. People are chasing each other, children are crying, women are yelling and screaming, abusing, and cursing everything, and every fly landing on their faces.

Both the young and the old are aged. Women are like men. Children's features have been older. Men have turned pale and have forgotten that they are men.

Hanging Bird Lane is located behind the Sultan's Palace in the Hamdin neighbourhood, which no one knows about or talks about anymore. It's a hot, hard, stale, barren lane with no heart, soul, or identity. A halfway lane, with none of the characteristics of the old lane that once existed.

There are, of course, people, but they had no shadows.

They have no past, no present, and indeed, no future. They are the dead, listed as living beings with no work, hope, sustenance, not a morsel of bread, no heartfelt laughter, not even a bashful smile.

Every day is torment, and every moment brings difficulty. Time is filled with inconvenience in this disgusting lane with the strange name of Hanging Bird Lane. No one knows or asks: Why? Why a bird? Why is it hanging?! And who hung it?! And, why!?

A small four-storey house, decrepit as everything else on the lane, stands at a corner of the lane where its erratic course ends. It is occupied by Al-Haja Kamela, the owner, who lives on the upper floor. Al-Haja Kamela wished she lived in a skyscraper, not because she is familiar with skyscrapers. She has no knowledge about them and has never even seen a picture of one in magazines or on satellite television. If you mentioned the word skyscraper to her, she might think you were talking about a mad mole, clawing at the air.

Nonetheless, Al-Haja Kamela dreams of living at the highest heights, the highest possible altitude. She is sick of the lane and its inhabitants and desires for God to grant her simple request since He is capable of anything.

She observes the residents from the top floor, watching their bustle, listening to their screams, invectives, and shrieks, nostalgic for a time when the people of Hanging Bird Lane were considered the epitome of genteelness, tolerance, generosity, cheerfulness, simplicity, and tenderness. What happened to all of that?

The people of Hanging Bird Lane began to despise one another and passers-by. Fathers despised their sons and daughters, as well as their brothers, their father's brothers, fathers, and their mother's brothers and all the females and males in the family. Of course, in this whirlpool, they do not forget that, naturally, they despise themselves. The lanes' residents love themselves so much and to such an extent that they end up on the other side of the issue and begin to hate themselves.

This exhausted Al-Haja Kamela and drove her to leave her home on the ground floor, where she had spent a lifetime, welcoming guests, family, loved ones, neighbours, and the people of the lane, being there for them, and sharing joys and sorrows with them. She enjoys their company; they are good people who soothe her heart and invigorate her sense of love.

It has been a long, long time. The situation has changed; the sieve has overturned, leaving nothing behind. With all the changes in the lane, Al-Haja Kamela lost the desire and ability to stay in direct contact with the situation all day and all night.

She left the ground floor to her only daughter when she was married off, and tenants occupied the first and second floors. She prefers them to be temporary tenants, staying there for short periods only for others to come and replace them. They leave, and others follow, and so on. She learned, through suffering, from former residents whom she was able to evict.

Al-Haja Kamela is sitting on an upholstered mattress which she sewed herself and stuffed with

white cotton that catches the eye and comforts
the body. She has a coffee pot in front of her and
cushions behind and around her back. She looks up at
God's vast sky, pondering the state of the world and
lamenting what has befallen people.

Only a few of those with whom she maintained
contact pay her visits. No one comes to her except
through her daughter, Naima. Naima dispatches one
of her sons or daughters to deliver the message about
the visit and the visitor. If Al-Haja Kamela likes the
person, she responds to the messenger with a sign,
and he or she passes it on to their mother to show
acceptance. Or another sign that Naima conceals as
she hesitates, looking at the visitor in the reception
room, giving the excuse that Al-Haja is sleeping. Even
though anyone who comes to visit Al-Haja will see
her overlooking surreptitiously from the upper floor
balcony when they get there and when they leave,
the matter is always decided by Al-Haja's whims
and moods.

Al-Haja is unaware of the twists and turns. "You
are one-eyed," she says to the one-eyed man's face.
However, she grows tired of meeting anyone missing
an eye, and experiences a strange sort of disgust if she
allows herself to meet them. Her disgust is reflected in
the words she utters during the visit of any one-eyed
man or woman. Being one-eyed means going against
your conscience or violating God's command and
surrendering to the will of the Devil within you.

Her younger, one-eyed sister, Sanniya, she is the
one-eyed person whom Al-Haja refused to see this
evening. She knows that the visit will cause her pain.

She is not tolerant of pain. She does not want to tell Sanniya again that she is fed up with her humiliating submission to her (nobody) husband, to whom she has surrendered for a long time and lost all the lightness, openness, cheerfulness, piety, and calmness of soul she was known for.

All of it vanished. Nothing remained of Sanniya except the dark, sluggish side that was dependent on the will of a man who lacked both a mind and a heart.

Kamela is aware that her sister, who hasn't visited her in months, will attempt to minimise the issue and turn the white into pitch black. And she will tell her a devious story, in a different and twisted form, that will recount how she did nothing wrong to Amal, and that a mother like her cannot be responsible for the suffering of the one whom she carried in her womb for nine months, loved and nursed her from her bosom and the yearning of her heart.

Al-Haja Kamela will grow tired of Sanniya's words and will contest them with her opinion for the thousandth time. She will beg Sanniya to tell the truth and put an end to the demonic act that has brought shame and disgrace to the family. Sanniya will cry and swear that Amal's stubbornness and refusal to respond to God Almighty's will is what truly brings her shame. Rather than strengthening Amal's heart for everyone, she will ask Kamela to be a good mediator. Al-Haja's heart will be tired, and she will lose her temper and heat up painful stings on her tongue for her sister, and she does not want any more grudges between her and Sanniya.

"Al-Haja is asleep!"

She is not sleeping or doing anything.

She simply wishes to be rid of her headache.

She doesn't want Sanniya's presence and arguments to remind her of all the humiliation her little sister has endured.

Kamela ruminates on a stock of old memories that time has not erased and, she believes, she cannot erase them. She is alone with herself in the isolation she imposed on herself and those around her, and facts and stories play out in her memories. Scenes, situations, words, and even suggestions without words or speech.

She had been consoling her younger sister Sanniya for a long time, first for her sin of marrying this man, and second for what was happening to her with no way to stop it.

"Ominous!"

This is what Al-Haja Kamela says to herself and sometimes shouts in Sanniya's face.

After the death of Al-Haja's mother, who could not live even for a month after fate had betrayed her and the angel of death had bereaved her of her man, time had ordained her to care for her sister.

Kamela will never forget her happy childhood and her father, the likes of whom are no longer found, and her mother who melted in love for him, and for the dust on his feet, because he was the man who honoured her and made her the lady of the house and of her life. So, she lived an honourable life, as she always said throughout her life with him, and after he went to meet his Lord.

He lived and died in Hanging Bird Lane when it was prestigious and famous, and loyalty, manliness, chivalry, hard work, generosity, and love for home and family were the measure of a man.

She sighs and sucks on her thick lips, which have now become rough. When the scorching air of memories touches her, she wonders, heartbroken, if there are any men like that left. Is there a single man now with even an ounce, a facade, a veneer, or an atom of my father's character?

The only ones in our affected lane are the likes of Adawi, her sister Sanniya's husband, who you can't put in the man category without feeling you're betraying this category, betraying the truth, betraying everything.

Kamela was relaxed. She recalls what happened as if it were happening right now, as if it had not been a year and a half. She stood in defiance of Adawi, condemning his barbaric behaviour against her sister and his seven daughters. The man was humiliated because all she had left behind were girls. He's been terrorizing his wife with various threats and menaces since the first girl was born, and that isn't enough for him; he eventually wanted to divorce her. He gave her the oath of divorce on the day she gave birth to her sixth daughter, Kamela, named after her aunt.

Aunt Kamela said to him, "Thank our Lord, Adawi, thank Him in all things for His grace. Girls are the world's adornment. They are the ones who give it flavour. Don't let silly thoughts take over your mind, else you'll end up putting your family in danger and forcing your wife and children to flee. Act like a man!

"Don't turn away from God's grace. Who knows, maybe the good you do them will be paid back to you later in your life. Just keep going forward, Adawi."

When confronted by Kamela, the Father of the Girls was confused. He stuttered and lost his ability to speak properly, blushing, and raving, with no choice but to retreat in defeat after expressing his disappointment, weakness, and self-humiliation by using all the crude phrases, insults, and miserable words he knows. He only got up to the door, slamming it forcefully after passing through it, and walked down Hanging Bird Lane, allowing his restless feet to carry him to the nearest café or a den located in a dark corner on the lane's outskirts. It's pitch black at all times of day and night.

Kamela recalls her bitter struggle with this freak, whom her sister Sanniya preferred to – and married over! – al-Usta Sayed, the lane's beloved taxi driver. Sanniya had already slept with Adawi without anyone's knowledge and she was feeling such unrivalled pleasure with him that she turned down al-Usta Sayed and others who asked for her hand without even thinking about her future, and how her future would have been better than the situation she was in if she had chosen any of them. "Frivolous!" Kamela muses to herself as she describes Sanniya, and she continues to ruminate on her. She wasted her life with this beast because she liked him in bed, as if the world had not provided her with another man who could make her happy in bed, and everywhere else.

Sanniya, of course, used her position as the family's youngest member, an orphan with no mother and no father, to put pressure on Kamela and Kamela's husband, as well as her other brothers and sisters. She was adamant about no discussion or intervention from any of them. She screamed at the top of her lungs with a rude tone, which she picked up because of her relationship with this creature and his support for her, that she would either marry Adawi or vanish from the face of the earth. News of her sinful relationship with this man, a man about whose profession, origin, or family background no one knew anything, leaked to everyone, including the inhabitants of the lane and Sanniya's family, but no one addressed the issue publicly. Kamela realized at the time that speaking about the scandal in public could have serious consequences for her family, and she was now the head of the family. This kept her from following the path of confrontation for which she was known in all her interactions, dealings, and relationships, and which she had never abandoned before.

Kamela was chastising herself at the time for her perceived indifference. She didn't want to give up one of her most important personality traits: masculinity.

However, she suffered a kind of defeat. It was difficult for her to be blamed by the family's men, women, boys, and girls for admitting, announcing, revealing, and exposing her younger sister, and to bring her family and its history to the ground with stupidity, impulsiveness, and utter folly, simply because she respected her politics, personality, and principles. And her masculinity!

Which principles compel a person to jeopardize their family's name and reputation, dignity, and future generations? What are the reasons, motives, logic, and wisdom that Kamela asserts?

Kamela would not be complete (the meaning of her name) if she had revealed Sanniya's scandal with Adawi.

Given this weak position, Sanniya gained brute force and married Adawi, whom everyone despises, and then she acquired all his traits, cheeky mannerisms, and roughness, replacing her pleasant disposition. She is no longer the sweet Sanniya, the generous Sanniya, the amusing Sanniya, or any of the others.

Adawi tried to bully Al-Haja at first, so his comeuppance was a headbutt. With part of his forehead crushed while his dignity was shattered.

Kamela shoved him against the wall, and in a sudden and decisive blow, her hard forehead hit his head, leaving his forehead unsound. It almost exploded. His head was about to disintegrate into shrapnel and crumbs. And he felt like he had died.

But he revived and went on to take tighter control of Sanniya, suppressing his rage, hoping that the right time would come for vengeance.

Although Al-Haja Kamela and everyone else in the house and lane, except for Sanniya, was mocking and despising him, he suppressed his anger and stilled himself, hoping that the right time would come to respond to everyone. What exactly would this response be? Nobody knows, and he has no idea. When will this happen? Nobody knows, including him.

***

Sanniya's life continued with Adawi, and Haja Kamela's and everyone else's attitude toward them remained unchanged. As a result, they packed their belongings and moved to another lane.

They were the parents to six daughters, and Adawi had devolved into a mindless ball of flesh and fat, bereft of feeling or essence, pursued by those who mocked him, not only because he was the Father of the Girls, but also because he had lost his masculinity and dignity with only his wife's sympathies in terms of money; money she would give him from time to time to satisfy his cravings and surrender to his drug addiction. When the kids' mother is at work, he does not leave the house for most of the day, and he avoids babysitting his daughters by holing up in his bedroom and consuming whatever opium he has. He despises his girls' inquiries about staying at home and not working. In the past, he used to tell them stories which insinuated that he was destined to never find anyone to employ him. Who would accept that a former manager, who used to give orders and reprimand his employees, would now work for them? He used to tell this story over and over, and his young girls believed he was telling the truth and that it was God's will.

But the girls grew up, learned what they learned, married who they married, and stayed at home, and the questions rang in his ears, dismissing his claims. He had no choice but to find a way out. Where would he go?

He spends the day sitting alone, wandering in the abyss. He refuses to leave the house because he is afraid that he will run into someone who will injure him and make him feel even more humiliated.

His daily life begins at night, after Sanniya's return. After amassing enough money to purchase more opium and lingering in cafes and dens, Adawi returns to be alone with his wife and make her happy. And he thinks that's all he's good for. But even having sex with the Mother of the Girls is no longer exciting. Neither of them feels any desire, making Adawi feel even more humiliated than usual because, as Sanniya says, he can't keep it up any longer.

***

His humiliation was palpable. He was humiliated at every turn in his confrontations with Kamela, whenever she ran into him, whenever fate decreed that they meet after the legendary headbutt, and fate had seemingly decreed that they must meet frequently. Add to that the humiliation and bitter scorn from which he rarely escapes without relapsing, the aggression of Alwad Mandour.

Sometimes a strange thought occurs to him that this Mandour is not a human, but a jinn sent by Satan himself to run roughshod over his existence and destroy it through physical and emotional challenges and fights.

With the failure of his attempts to eliminate all of this through kindness, politeness, and withdrawing from any clash or friction, and after he became tired of it all, he told his wife Sanniya to prepare to move to another house, or even another lane, and leave Hanging Bird Lane, because it no longer provides him with comfort, stability, or reassurance.

Sanniya is also living under the curse of her sister's refusal to interact with or greet her, and her reputation has been shattered in the eyes of her daughters, one of whom approaches her and tells her she despises living in Hanging Bird Lane and cannot stand its inhabitants. "It's as if we're criminals or insane, as if no one thinks we're human."

She reluctantly agrees to leave the lane where she was born and has spent her entire life.

But there's a bigger problem than that!

Where should I go?

Sanniya sits alone, attempting to find a suitable location, absorbed in her thoughts.

She unwinds.

Hanging Bird Lane is everything to Sanniya, her birthplace, family and friends, girls, boys, and women, school, adolescence, competing for men with her female peers, because she had no future without one. *Men provide more shelter than walls, a woman is nothing without a man* and *the measure of a man is his wallet.*

A strange shop stood at one of the corners of the lane, neither above nor below ground. You enter it by descending a slope parallel to some stairs. The store is virtually beneath but actually adjacent to the house's entrance, separated only by a brick railing to rest on. Sanniya's life had been turned upside down at this gloomy shop a few steps from her home because of its location and the owner's miserliness. She was a high school student who was quiet, nice, courteous, and shy, as anyone who knew her would tell you. So, the shop owner's son, Adawi, fell in love with her. He met her several times when she came asking after his father, al-Haj Darwish. Adawi worked in a laundry and the shop owner was his father.

Sanniya did not believe Adawi was the right person for her because she was educated, and he was ignorant. She was to attend university and become a teacher, a lawyer, or even a respectable employee, while he would remain an ironing boy. He may eventually become the shop's owner. Did Sanniya want to be the wife of an ironing man in the future, with all her hopes, dreams, and visions for herself and her future?

This question, and her negative response, shaped her attitude toward Adawi. She treated him with reluctance and loftiness, with courage and harshness when she was bold; she ignored him in front of his father, al-Haj Samahi, and the boys who work for him.

However, this situation did not last long, as the group of her teen girls secretly sought to win a man (a young man from the lane).

Sanniya had only one option: Adawi. The remaining males were either drafted or worked in dangerous jobs that required them to be present only at night, whereas the girls in the lane did not leave their homes at night.

There were, of course, those who were significantly older or significantly younger. But this was not the only reason Sanniya became involved with this Adawi. What occurred was beyond her control, and if the matter had been in her hands, it wouldn't have happened. Adawi took advantage of Sanniya coming into the shop while he was alone in it. Al-Haj Samahi, his father, was absent and out on an errand, and the laundry boy who was supposed to come to help Adawi, as al-Haj had said while leaving the shop, did not come, and would never come.

Someone came to inform al-Haj of the situation, but he only found Adawi. Then Sanniya appeared, inquiring about al-Haj Samahi, because her father had sent her there. She walked into the store and Adawi pulled down the metal door that was wrapped up and raised to the top, rolling it down to the ground level. A garage door. The shop was originally a garage before the house's owner transformed it into its current form.

This metal shutter wrapped up under the shop sign is often pulled down, and the residents and customers of the lane know that Al Haj has gone on an errand, or that he didn't even leave the house, or that the boy who was responsible for opening the shop today hasn't arrived yet.

Adawi encircled Sanniya and began to speak softly to her about her sweetness, wit, taste, and beauty. All of this had no direct result because she was annoyed, tense, and distressed by this silly boy's behaviour. She was determined to open the door or else scream, and the whole world would blame him.

Adawi laughed as he explained to her that no one would hear her shrieking at the top of her lungs. The metal shutter was soundproof.

He promised her that he would not cause her any harm or trouble of any kind and declared the love and admiration he had had for her since the first time he saw her with her friends, and that he had no intention of harming her as long as he felt that way about her.

She began to relax. She was overcome with relief because someone cared about her, flirted with her, and did not intend to offend her. She was overcome with the strange sensation that she had accomplished her desired goal—winning a man. And she imagined herself bragging to her classmates about being the only one who had won the secret race!

The sense of relief grew into a sense of pride and brilliance. She surrendered to him and his love, despite her mind's warnings to stay away from those she saw as less than her, a laundry boy.

She returned that day to inform her father that al-Haj was not at the shop.

Her father yelled at her, "He's gone, and you've been gone for an hour. Where have you been all this time, girl?"

Sanniya was scared and told him that she had met one of her classmates and got tied up in a conversation with her about some study matters, and that she was sorry.

Her father forgave her. If he had known she had spent all this time with the Adawi boy inside the closed shop, this would have been her last day on earth.

Her friends surrounded her with jealous looks and pursued her with questions in the schoolyard at breaktime when Sanniya told the four girls about her great achievement and winning a boy.

Tafida, the pickle vendor's daughter, swaying disapprovingly, said, "How did you do it, girl? Tell us about it."

Sanniya told the story, and the girls in the surrounding circle transformed into wax statues. The heat of the encounter and the adventure with the Adawi boy nearly melted these wax statues. Questions, comments, and laughter flew. The matter raised questions, such as, "did everything happen?".

Samara, the group's eldest and most lustful member, and the most talkative about sex at their gatherings, posed the probing question.

Sanniya responded that she was not exactly sure what had happened. Although the question fuelled her desire, she deliberately responded like that.

The youngest girl in the group, Nousa, was more concerned with another matter: "Can we say congratulations in advance? When will the party be, my dear? Will we be invited?"

Sanniya feels pride and superiority, and she perceives jealousy, envy, and a lot of respect in the eyes of her friends, their expressions, and movements. She says, "Everything happens in its own time, my dear Noussy. Everything happens in its own time."

"One more thing, miss."

Amani, the principal's daughter, chanted politely with a hint of irony: "Is this Adawi? Isn't he beneath you, Sounsoh? Didn't you tell us once that after you finish university, you'll find yourself a husband and that he should be of the same standing as you, a doctor or a professor?"

Sanniya was confused and could not find a way out except to say that she was still young and didn't know what to do but enjoy what she has in her hand, and a bird in the hand is better than ten in the bush.

Tafidah, the pickle vendor's daughter, laughed before saying, "I'm thinking of you and the other members of the group. All of us need a significant other. Each of them will have to take her in their arms. A girl has no other option but to marry. I mean, education isn't more important than attachment."

Amani, the principal's daughter, was against it.

"What kind of nonsense are you talking, Tuftuf? Do you believe that every girl is like you and that no one has anything but a man on her mind?"

***

Sanniya recalls how Adawi charmed her and made her set aside his flaws and low social and educational status (he dropped out of middle school to work in his father's shop). Adawi started dealing with her body and teaching her the significance of her possession of her body, making her blossom and explode with feelings of becoming distinct, brilliant, and feminine.

When something naughty happened, she just surrendered herself to him and enjoyed the sensual pampering and instinctive lust. Sanniya changed. She began to deteriorate. She went insane and lost interest in everything.

She had outperformed her classmates in attracting a man, but she could not continue her secondary education. She broke down after succumbing to the sex addiction she secretly indulged in with Adawi.

Her deterioration and breakdown were exacerbated by her father's death. She felt lost and that Adawi and no one else could save her. He would eventually become the shop's owner, sooner or later.

Sanniya was now drowning in a well of regret, cursing herself, her disappointment, and her circumstances.

Her competitors, whom she had defeated, continued their studies, and even those who did not finish high school got jobs in businesses, shops, and companies. Those who attended universities went on to hold more prestigious positions. One is now an account manager, another is a lawyer, and the third holds a doctorate from the College of Education. What happened to you, Sanniya, and why do you have such bad luck?

It wasn't bad luck at all. She is aware that she strayed from the start, that she has lost her ability to stand out. She lost her compass, and her father had died, so she had lost someone who was supporting her and taking care of her education, leaving her with only her eldest sister, Kamela.

But Kamela cannot afford to pay for Sanniya's education; she can only support herself and her family, and she cannot even provide Sanniya with pocket money regularly. She had to take care of everything. Adawi, now the owner of the shop, was her sole support. When he first asked her to be a partner in the shop, she decided to marry him against the wishes of Kamela and the rest of the family.

She lived in Adawi's apartment between two fires, trying to find meaning in her life though everything was lost and over.

Both were living in an old house in the lane, near to the shop, and the apartment was an old one that

Adawi inherited from his father. There are no other heirs. His mother died before his father, and he was his parents' only child.

Of course, Adawi could not teach her his profession, so she lived with no work except being in the shop, and her husband began to feel the difficulty of the role that he was suddenly forced to play as a shop owner. He escaped it by relying on his workers, and with time, he stopped caring about anything other than earning an income every day and spending most of what he earned on drugs so that he could continue his nightly duties with his wife efficiently, as he imagined; and it did not take long before he got in trouble, landed in debt, and was on the verge of bankruptcy.

He was adamant that Sanniya give birth to a son. This resulted from his need for someone to support him in his work and livelihood, and he would fill the void left by his loss of solitude. There are no parents, owners, or sons, only girls, girls, girls!

Sabrieh, an elderly woman from the lane, paid her a visit in the shop one day, an unexpected and unusual visit, given that most of the shop's customers were men, young men, or girls sent by their elders.

Everything will be all right if God wills.

The woman sat silently, asking no questions, and carrying no clothes for ironing.

Sabrieh attempted to approach Sanniya about something she wanted to say to her, but she did not find the right moment, as customers came and Adawi left, leaving Sanniya to bear the entire burden, supervising the workers, talking with customers, and struggling to keep the shop going.

Both agreed that she would come to the house in the evening. Sanniya had no idea what the old woman wanted to tell her or open to her about. Sabrieh kept the secret, contenting herself to say that it was something good, God willing, but it requires secrecy and is not appropriate to discuss openly, as anyone might overhear!

Sanniya didn't know how to interpret Sabrieh's mysterious words. What does this old woman, with whom I have no relationship and whom I only see every now and then, want?

Evening arrived, Sabrieh arrived, and Sanniya's patience had worn thin. She knows that this woman has been widowed for years and worked at houses to raise her children, and the children grew up and became men and women, and some are still alive, while others have died or migrated, and there is only one girl left living with her in the lane. She works in one of the nearby schools, and there was no decent man who would accept her as a wife. She is now an old maid. So, what exactly does she want from me? And what is the problem that means we need secrecy and to keep away from anyone, who might overhear their conversation?!

Sabrieh explained, "My dear, I am aware of the barbaric situation you are in, which is why I first thought of you. I have a job for you that offers daily food, a place to sleep, and shelter until our Lord, God willing, gives you and Adawi salvation. What do you say?"

Sanniya listened in utter silence to the old woman's long speech about her desire to quit her job due to her age and inability to meet its requirements, and her desire for Sanniya to take her place. She was listening in complete silence, while recalling thoughts and memories about her teenage ambitions, and her aspirations to overcome the suffering she was experiencing in the lane.

The old woman's unexpected offer stunned her, and the woman received nothing but silence in response!

She was also embroiled in an internal conflict:

Is this what will become of her in the end? A servant in other people's homes? If she had listened to Kamela's words, valued herself, and looked forward, the situation would have been different, she thought to herself before deciding how to respond. Then she decided to decline this offer straight away.

Sabrieh assured her that she was free to choose, but cautioned her not to lose sight of the fact that this was a once-in-a-lifetime opportunity. And that the people in the house where she would work are good people and would treat her as if she were their daughter.

When the old woman sensed Sanniya's psychological turmoil, she advised her to think about it calmly for a reasonable amount of time. Then she bid her farewell and promised to return in a day or two. She walked out of the apartment. Sanniya sat back down on the sofa and brewed herself another cup of tea. She was mulling the idea over, on the verge of tears.

But she couldn't make up her mind. The salary she would receive was very appealing – it would meet or exceed the needs of her, her husband, and their only daughter, Shama.

But, at the end of the day, would Sanniya work as a maid?

When Adawi arrived before the end of Sanniya's long day, she could not tell him about the situation and discuss it with him, even though she was convinced that he would agree without reservation. She chose to forget everything today and immerse herself in a sea of pleasure, maybe to escape her deteriorating circumstances. Sex is Sanniya's drug.

Sanniya had no idea when or how Adawi agreed to accept the idea of working at a house. She had to have been high on drugs; she had to have been on another planet; there had to have been something.

Did he tell her that the work would be temporary, until things improved, and they would no longer require it, they wouldn't have accepted if their circumstances had been better?

Did he tell her that she would be working as a house manager rather than a maid? I mean, you'd be a manager. A manager, Sanniya, for a long time?

The important thing is that she responded and accepted, and when she told Sabrieh, the woman almost flew with joy. She promised to tell the madam right away, and Sanniya couldn't believe it when she heard herself accept.

A maid, in the end, Sanniya?!

And because she knows that Adawi is a failure in every way except one, and that after he lost his father and the shop, and after the bankruptcy and debts, a solution must be found, and the solution is in her hands. She had to forget all her ambitions and perceptions of herself, burying her dreams in the cemetery of bitter reality.

She was defeated, and she has agreed to work as a maid in other homes to save her home.

She was certain that Adawi would not be decisive, and that his promise to improve the situation so that she would not have to serve in the houses was merely a ploy to take the pressure off her, and she was powerless to prevent herself from sinking into this abyss.

A maid, Sanniya?!

Kamela nearly collapsed and fell to the ground, landing on her chest and moaning as if someone close to her had died.

She tried to dissuade her from accepting the offer. She tried to think of a profession or job that she could apply to or find through her many contacts with property owners and shop owners.

Adawi, Sanniya told her, promised her that the job as a maid would not last long and that he would find a job.

With bitter irony, Kamela responded, "Die then, you moron!"

Despite her sadness over her little sister's disappointment, she said aloud to herself, "Will she live on Adversary's handouts? Is that what you're telling me, dear sister? But what if your mind is completely occupied and you can't see anything else?!"

***

The man transitions from job to job, then to unemployment, then to work that appears to be unemployment, and finally to being unemployed without work. And Sanniya's conditions in terms of job opportunities and fields of work, despite distress and constraint, were far superior to his. She could work in homes, serving, cooking, washing, cleaning, and caring for young children while their parents were at work. Sanniya pays the price for her insistence on Adawi, as well as her disdain for and violation of all popular Egyptian norms and principles. She works and suffers at all hours of the day in the service of the people who provide her family and daughters with their livelihood. She also suffers at home while caring for the girls and their father, who is mostly supported by her.

Adawi is not ashamed of the fact that he survives off his wife's job. He remains in his state and spends most of his time, day, and night, in the company of other drug addicts.

Sanniya believes she is the source of all the adversity, grief, misery, and despair she encounters. She accepts the situation and ignores the agonizing paradox that her man's livelihood comes from her work, not the other way around.

Because sex is her only pleasure, she spends all her time on it when she is not working in people's homes. It is her marijuana and her opium that Adawi provides for her; he has no control over anyone but her.

Sanniya sometimes feels as if she is living a lustful life with a man rather than a marital life. She pays him the price for his achievements in bed.

As time passes, the number of girls increases, there are new mouths to feed, and the burden of providing the means for their survival, food, shelter, and clothing, falls on this crushed, toiling woman.

Sanniya realizes that any attempt to improve her condition or her life is futile. She felt filled with a victorious feeling in the early years of her marriage to this creature, who was despised by everyone around him. She had what she desired. None of her family members approved of their marriage. The reason is straightforward: her husband, who unjustifiably clings to her, has no work, no family, no address, no qualifications, no profession, no job, no anything!

Al-Haja Kamela, her older sister, explained to her that this Adawi, the man for whom she will not even look at another, has no morals or conscience, and that he endangers her life and future.

Sanniya was clinging to him with insane tenacity. Her secret relationship with him enthralled her.

Although in rare, fleeting moments she was aware of the truthfulness of what Kamela and the others said, the lustful obsession that plagued her painted a different picture for her, and the truth hid behind her in shame.

Arrogance, ignorance, and succumbing to the whirlpool of pleasure all close the doors to reason, prudence, intellect, and sound judgment. But she realized that what she was doing was the essence of her mind because she, and only she, knew what she wanted and who she loved.

Adawi, or death, she decided impetuously.

And when Sanniya thinks clearly in some fleeting and unintentional moments, she admits to herself, and only herself, that this was the mistake of her life, that she has been paying for it over the years, and she cannot turn back the clock, nor does she have a will strong enough to allow her to put her life back on track. She wants to start a new life with a human being free from Adawi's everlasting infirmity. A man in the true sense of the word, not just an animal who was useless outside of the bed.

Sanniya swallowed her disappointment and cried for herself in solitude. Where does she get her determination? And where is a man willing to marry a mother of seven daughters (in fact) and six daughters and a son by her own accounts, as well as Adawi's accounts, the man she wishes to get rid of, but cannot. Sanniya has been defeated, and she now lives like a bull turning its waterwheel, spinning, spinning, spinning, without hope or meaning, indefinitely.

What is tiring is that she is obstinate, finds flaws, and insists that she is correct and that Adawi does not have all the flaws and shortcomings that he is labelled with. True, he is deficient, but not to that extent, and is there even such a thing as a perfect human being?

SECOND STAGE

The pleasure of leaving everything behind!

Sanniya is completely perplexed.

She and her husband are hoping their seventh child will be a boy, a crown prince. He will mature into a man worthy of the family name.

Adawi has other considerations; what irritates him are the whips of insult and ridicule that he receives every hour of every day, the Father of the Girls has arrived, the Father of the Girls. The Father of the Girls.

He is now chastising himself for not being harsh with Sanniya when she made her first mistake. If he had done what he had determined to do and divorced her, he would have been happy, with another wife who would bear sons for him. He needs a son, a man, a male who will share the burden with him and shield him from the curse of the Father of the Girls that had befallen him. If he had resolved to divorce Sanniya at that time, she would not have given birth to this barn full of girls, and even the seventh girl, Amal, whom he and Sanniya attempted to make a son. A midwife,

Sithom, assisted them. She grew up and showed
signs of femininity; her chest rounded, her buttocks
rounded, she gained softness, silkiness, and litheness,
but he and Sanniya insisted she was a boy!

As for Sanniya, she went through a difficult
period after the birth of each girl. Adawi desired a son
every time.

After the ill-treatment, cruelty, and harshness with
which Adawi treated her following the birth of their
first daughter, Shama, she considered divorce from
Adawi, although it would have been painful, but, as
her sister Al-Haja Kamela reiterated, it is a blessing in
disguise. Who knows, she might begin a new life with
a suitable man whose mind is not preoccupied with
the myth of boys and girls. Perhaps she would find
someone who comforts her, treats her well, and who
would not harass her simply because she bears girl
after girl.

She succumbed to her husband's pressure. She
calmed herself down and told herself in her heart that
Amal was a boy. When she thinks back on what she
said, she realizes she was talking about her new-born,
in a female conscience!

Is this because all she left behind were daughters?

Is it because she knows the seventh child is
also a girl!?

She falls into the well of confusion.

She spends a lot of time talking to herself. Adawi
is constantly absent from the house because it is clear
from his speech and actions that he despises the girls
and is upset even with their mother, and he claims

that the fault lies with her and what she has given him. Sanniya almost always cries, but her sufferings taught her to cry silently, without shedding tears, so what did her tears bring her but more endless agony? And he is absent even when he is present inside the house. Staying withdrawn mostly, or drowning in the well of drugs from which he hardly ever emerges until he falls back to its bottom. If Sanniya knew anything about the Greek mythology of Sysyphus, she would not hesitate to refer to her husband Adawi as Sysyphus (or perhaps it would be easier to refer to him as shitty-phus), with the difference, of course, that Sysyphus used to carry the rock and ascend the mountain with it, and then it would fall and roll back down the mountain, and he would follow it up and down to infinity.

Adawi hardly wakes up from the effects of the drugs, whether it is hashish or opium, he just falls into his deep well and stays there for a long time at the bottom, absent all the times, except on rare occasions.

***

Nothing can stop time, and as it passes, Adawi's situation worsens. With the stability and even improvement of Sanniya's work conditions and income, her voice became louder, and Adawi withdrew himself into a corner. His presence faded away, and his disappointment grew.

She had no choice but to take care of her six daughters.

And the seventh, her son Amal.

And if it weren't for her fear that everyone would regard her as a detestable, vicious woman who would harm her daughter, the last of the bunch, Amal, she would abandon the ploy that Adawi had devised for her with the help of the midwife Sithom, and openly admit that she had taken part in a heinous crime against the dearest beloved, the last of the bunch.

Amal, our daughter.

But she refuses to admit it. Her fear always wins, but unexpectedly, courage appears to her.

Sanniya deteriorated over time, and she missed her early days and years with Adawi, the pleasant life and constant sex. She had liked that. And she felt that her femininity brought her happiness, because sex was the only meaning of happiness in her own dictionary.

When Adawi was at the pinnacle of his glory, she was at the pinnacle of her happiness, and when he was performing poorly in bed and became weak because of his feelings of inability to fulfil his obligations and inability to get a constant, secure, and sustained job with an earning that fulfilled the obligations he had, Sanniya's happiness started shrinking and dwindling and disappearing, and instead depression, violence, disgust, and hatred set in. Sanniya felt she had squandered her life with this arrogant man named Adawi, and that she was stupid, a fool, and a slut who only thought about what was between her thighs.

She muttered to herself, wondering if this rich man, who drives the latest models of cars and travels abroad on vacations, pays huge fees for his children to attend foreign schools, and pays me a monthly salary equivalent to that of a respected employee. If this gentleman who lives in and owns a luxury villa, has a summer chalet on the Mediterranean Sea and another on the Red Sea and throws parties in the luxury villa where he lives or outside of it, he is obviously an educated man with a university degree. This man thinks I'm beautiful and sexy, although he looks like a movie star, knows respected men, and discusses politics and major issues. What will I lose if I give myself up to him?

How stupid was I when I decided to marry this idiot, Adawi?!

Why shouldn't I try to please my master? He will satiate my desire, accentuate my femininity, quench my thirst, and fill my pockets. Who knows, maybe things will develop more with him. Who knows?

When Sanniya finished her work in Elwan's villa and was preparing to make the long journey back from Zamalek to her lane in the Hamidin neighbourhood, she heard "ahem", and was surprised by her master above her head, as she bent over and picked up her belongings from the bathroom floor, while drying her hair after a sneaky shower in the luxurious bathtub.

Elwan had arrived earlier than usual. There was no one in the villa at this hour. The kids were at school, their mother was at work, and she—Sanniya—had completed everything the Madam had asked of her. Mr Elwan. She could have waited a half-hour or more for the Madam to return, but she preferred to get home sooner. She had a strong desire to sleep and rest. Sanniya had grown tired of cleaning the house, and his voice consoled her.

"Where are you going, girl? I arrived early just for you. I'd like to say something to you."

"Is it alright, Mr Elwan?"

"Of course, Souny, come with me to the living room."

Sanniya was not comfortable with his pampering of her. But an expectation filled her that he was going to do something unusual. What? She didn't know. She resisted her wild desire to find out what it would be right away. She would be patient for a while and everything would become clear.

Her movements insinuated to Elwan that she was ready for what he had in store for her, and he approached her as if smelling the fragrance of her body. In more than one stolen moment he had previously hinted at things. Her luscious, radiant body moved at the pace of a woman fascinated by her own femininity, and it took her longer than usual to get from the bathroom to the living room. She was sauntering. This was not lost on Elwan. He was confident that whatever he told her would be accepted without question.

He sat very relaxed on his favourite sofa, and he told her, "Listen, I mean, you're tired of working at home and all this heartache, and I want to comfort you so you can relax, so I've arranged for you to live as a lady of leisure. What do you think, Sounsoun?"

"My God, I'm exhausted. This is what I had been dreaming of for ages, and I had thought to ask your permission to look for someone to replace me."
She stopped halfway through her complaint and

asked him, "But what arrangement do you have in mind, sir?"

"I keep calling you Souny and Sounsoun, but you address me as Sir."

"Shouldn't I address you as Sir?"

"What if you call me, my Elwan?"

Sanniya laughed loudly, closed her eyes, and threw herself onto the sofa next to him.

"Oh, my Elwan, I'll call you my Elwan!"

"I'm falling in love with you, and I've set aside an apartment in my building for you. I want you to stay there and not work or tire yourself."

"What am I supposed to do in this apartment?"

"You don't have to do anything. Instead of coming here during working hours, you'll go there and prepare until I arrive."

Elwan rose from his seat, leaned in, and grabbed her cheeks while saying, "Shouldn't something as sweet as you are be kept from hardship? Don't you have the right to be cherished, adored, to feel your spirit, and to meet someone who understands and appreciates your worth?"

During his speech, his palms loosened and reached out to Sanniya's charms, her round flesh. He had stopped speaking at that point, and his lips were touching hers.

Sanniya resisted, or rather pretended to resist. She was aflame on the inside; her victory fuelled every beat of her fleeing body.

For a long time, she remained silent, her head fluttering in confusion: What does this pampering and caressing mean for me?

He snapped her out of her reverie with a quick kiss, threw himself on her chest and said, "You will enjoy comfort and we will have a customary marriage that only you me and the bedpost will know about."

"What sweet talk is this?" she said.

She could not believe her ears as she ran her fingers through his hair. She could not think of anything to say. She remained silent.

Another long kiss, which she responded to so fluently, made him feel as if he needed nothing else from her.

The situation would have escalated if it had not been for the sounds of chaos outside the door of the villa. But it was, of course, cut short. The Madame had arrived with the boys.

Elwan said that Sanniya was tired and promised to drive her home himself. He yanked her behind him quickly.

Ihab, his son, said, "How did she get tired? She's tough as an elephant, Daddy. Didn't you know?"

He did not look at him or listen to him. He rushed out of the door.

All the details were worked out along the way. Sanniya raised no objections. She did not, however, express her agreement with anything.

She was in conflict within herself, consenting and happy but dismissive and afraid of the consequences. In an instant, she feels victorious, feels herself entering a world she has never imagined or ever imagined less than. A stifled euphoria intoxicates her, draws her into a panic.

Do you believe this is heaven, Sanniya, or
hell on fire?

She had no choice but to obey her master, Elwan,
whose daring move of taking her for a ride in his
luxury car surprised her. She had only seen it from
afar, and she did not know how much she would enjoy
a trip in it. And she is even more surprised by Elwan's
daring in claiming that she is tired, and her surprise
grows to the point of fascination when she considers
the specifics of what he's offered her. What does he
expect from me?

His own angelic mistress, or a secret second wife?

Is he interested in me? Is he in love with me? Is it a
fun game? And with so much money?

Of course, he knows that I am not on his level.
I'm not as well educated as he is. But why the idea of
customary marriage? He could have simply enjoyed
me with his money, without an engagement, if he
so desired. I'm not sure. It was a strange mystery. It
required an explanation.

Elwan noticed that Sanniya was careless and
distracted, and he suspected what was going on in
her head. He asked her, "Do you want to go to the
building and see your apartment?"

She responded with phoney rage. "Just because
it's me, I'll agree!? Why don't you give me a chance to
think, my Elwan?"

He detected a hint of pampering in her response,
so he replied, "So, until you have a plan, let it be next
time. Sounsoun, please."

She requested to be dropped off near the main
street where she lives. She asked to be dropped off in

one of its lanes, not wanting to be seen getting out of a fancy car driven by a good-looking man.

***

Sanniya pondered and understood and needed no further thought; she wanted to escape the blazing fire burning in her every day, and to fly to Elwan's paradise. Three daughters had grown up and had three husbands, and God had taken two of them, perhaps out of compassion for them or their parents! Except for Rida, none of them stayed. No one knows the whereabouts of Amal. Sanniya, though she never admits it to anyone, deep down, knows she is a girl, but she feels compelled to say that she is a boy, and she defies her sister, the eldest in the family, Al-Haja Kamela, who insists she is a girl and threatens Sanniya with hellfire as a punishment for this crime.

Will the fires of Hell consume me? It is burning me, and I am the oppressed fool in all this satanic nonsense. Why did I give in to Adawi's cursed desire?

Why did I put my precious daughter in this horrible, never-ending prison? I am the perpetrator, and the fire is pursuing me. I need to get away from all of this pain. Elwan is the promised land. I'm going to paradise so the fires of hell can scorch Adawi.

Sanniya still has one question unanswered: Why a customary marriage?!

Elwan was not surprised when she found an opportunity to confront him with the question. He said it without hesitation, without waiting, with the answer on the tip of his tongue:

"Oh, Sounsoun, my darling, the situation does not call for a question. I want to protect your rights on your behalf. I am an honest man who does not mince words, and if it weren't for the circumstances, I would have made an official contract with you, but for the time being, let us make it customary in the Way of God and His Messenger until the time is right. Is that clear?"

Sanniya was taken aback by this. She thought, this is a respectable man, this man doesn't play around. Alwan keeps me safe!

***

During their first meeting in the flat he assigned to her in his building, Elwan explained to her that he does not like anything illegal and will not accept his influence or money being used to achieve what he desires, and this is the secret of his determination to have a legal relationship with her, in the form of a customary marriage.

While undressing, except for a luxurious nightgown he had purchased for her among the clothes and other items that she had discovered there, she said amorously, "But, my dear, my dear, you forgot something crucial."

"What?"

"You forgot I'm married. I mean, I'm still in Adawi's custody."

"No, I forgot nothing. I am aware, and I also know that we will resolve this issue as soon as possible, by mutual consent."

"And what about work now?"

"There is no reason to. We are in love. We can do what we want."

"Well, what about Adawi?"

"We must deal with him as soon as possible. Seek divorce from him legally and agree to anything."

She had left the chair she was sitting in and went to the chaise longue, where Alwan was lying relaxed, and stripped off most of his clothes, so he was almost naked. She clung to him and felt calm, and the thought that she had passed from one world to another entered her mind.

There was no other option but to get rid of Adawi.

Adawi didn't realize it for some reason and found himself pondering!

He usually lives his life day by day, moment by moment, with nothing on his mind. He does not damage his mind by overthinking. He is happy and at peace most of the time unless he cannot find work or loses his job. He doesn't keep himself busy. He has spent most of his life – and he is now over fifty – drugged, his empowerment. He stuffs opium under his tongue in his mouth and gives it (life) only a sip. He is unconcerned about anything. He is unconcerned about himself. He is only concerned with making Sanniya happy in bed. After that, she gets worked up, thinks a lot, and grieves for her husband's condition, although she has never had to worry about losing her job because she is always needed for domestic service work. and the house in which she serves pays her well.

As a result, Adawi is happy, and his mind is free of anxiety, thoughts, and fears of the betrayal of time, despite suffering severe attacks of ridicule and insults from the frequent visitors of the dens, who almost always stay there, especially Mandour, who never leaves him alone. He stings him with sharpened words and remarks: Father of the Girls. Sanniya is suffering and toiling for the sake of money, and Adawi needs dosh (hashish dosh), every day.

Adawi frequently fights with Mandour and is often defeated by him. However, he fights again and again. With each defeat, he prefers to remain silent and claim wisdom, relying on those who stand up to Mandour and object to his stings and ridicule. But defeat is defeat, clear as the sun, and the crowd's objection in one den or another, and Mandour's submission to their defence, does not turn Adawi's defeat into a victory.

Adawi was suddenly caught up in a state of thought!

He had noticed many changes in Sanniya recently and for a long time.

"Sanniya, you've changed a lot, my God," he says to himself in an audible voice, sitting in the far corner of the den, sucking on a significant piece of opium with star anise.

Years before, she had felt old. She didn't care about her appearance or posture, and she didn't laugh, gossip, sing, or hum like she used to. He used to tell himself that he knew why he hadn't asked her.

He knows that he is the cause.

He was no longer the Adawi she used to make any excuse to visit in his cabin on the roof of a dilapidated house for mutual pleasure! This was done in secret, without her family's knowledge, and before their marriage, which took place against the wishes of Al-Haja Kamela, her older sister, the head of her family, and her guardian.

Again, on another day, Adawi ponders.

"But one day, she came to you early, and she wasn't as happy as she had been in the past. Sanniya changed. She started neglecting herself. She was no longer waiting for you eagerly.

"And you, Adawi," he says audibly to himself while sitting alone in a solitary corner of the den—"you, Adawi, you achieved salvation. You are of no use, neither in bed nor anywhere. Your daughters are useful throughout the house. Some of them work, some of them learn, and one of them is still young and unemployed, awaiting her turn. But you, Adawi, you are saved! No jobs or activities. You lazy bum. But where does Sanniya fit in?"

Sanniya has changed. She had changed more in the last two days than she had at first. She was still conscious of herself, her figure, her eyebrows, her gait, and her speech, and her gaze changed, Oh, Adawi.

The man sitting in the corner of the den, talking to himself in a broken voice, had transformed into a man mourning himself, just as women do at funerals.

He has nothing of his own, no work, no income, nothing. He survives day-to-day on the money he can take by abusing the kindness of his working wife (she has already been changing a lot for a while now) or one of his working daughters.

He finds no refuge to escape from all of this except for dens, hashish, and opium, and, while he often encounters only difficulties and insults there, particularly from Mandour, the pleasure of leaving everything behind and being completely alone is always—and especially now—unrivalled.

Adawi fell into the well of thoughts, and though he dislikes thinking, he flees it like someone escaping a bloodthirsty beast. This time, he could not flee. He fell between the beast's fangs and wondered, what happened to Sanniya? She changed once, and then changed again.

Adawi knows, or he is aware of, but ignores, what is happening to Sanniya or what she has been concealing from him for quite some time. When he went to follow her from the moment she left the house in the morning, he concluded that he couldn't confront her with what he had discovered.

He went ahead of her, going out and then standing back and watching the house from a distance.

Sanniya went out wearing full make-up, which is a departure from her usual practice of many years. She continues her usual path, coming from deep inside the lane to the bus station that will take her to her workplace. Adawi hides, and after she boards the bus with the other passengers, he jumps in at the last second.

She arrives at her station. He gets off after a few moments, without her noticing.

She walks the way women from the nice neighbourhood walk, a gait her husband is unfamiliar with, a gait with a greater sense of self. The gait of madams.

Adawi does not know what this is all about. How does a maid walk with a gait that only madams have?

After a while, he realizes she has not gone to the house of Elwan Bek, whom he knows well, since the time when he would visit Sanniya, either to make her feel as if he was guarding and protecting her, or to ask for money if he suddenly became penniless or needed more money, or simply to spy on her.

He had stopped making these visits a long time ago, when she warned him that if he continued with them, her livelihood would be cut off.

"And now, Sanniya, where are you going? Did Elwan and his family move to a house other than the villa I know about? You didn't tell me that."

She walked into a large building, greeted the door attendant, and he returned the greeting. She entered the elevator. Adawi moved as the elevator moved. He approached the door attendant and inquired about the building's owner, as he had an interest in him. The door attendant told him that the owner's name was Elwan al-Malwani.

"Does he live here? Can I, like, meet him?"

"Sure, why not?"

"What do you mean?"

"He has a large villa, but he has an apartment here. At times, he spends hours here."

Adawi understood everything.

But will he confront Sanniya?

He pondered and pondered and returned to one of his favourite dens to give himself a chance to think deeply and mull it over.

"What do you stand to gain by confronting Sanniya, my brother?" A part of his mind that is susceptible to hashish and opium inquired, and Adawi could not provide a useful response. His thoughts were racing between the possibility that his wife would reveal the secret to him and request a divorce, and the possibility that she would tell him a lie and conceal the truth, and he couldn't tell her he was spying on her or following her without her knowing. Her only option would be to file for divorce. He was the one who had threatened her with divorce at the time because of the large number of daughters she had given birth to. So, who is the winner now?

"Sanniya, you beast."

He said to himself that, deep down, he meant you idiot.

He was too frail to take any action that would cause the loss of his privilege: a life of unemployment, freedom, and getting high.

With one word, he could lose everything. He would lose Sanniya and the money she spends on him, as well as the apartment he shares with her and the other girls and everything else.

But the cat within him fell into a well of curiosity, a desire to know about Sanniya and what had happened to her. What exactly was she up to?

The opium melted in his mouth, but the question did not leave his tongue or his mind.

Through his investigations and monitoring of his wife's movements, Adawi learned some information, although most of it was uncertain and vague. The most important thing is that Sanniya does not work in Elwan Bek's villa, as she claims, but spends the entire day in an apartment in a building owned by the Bek!

What is she doing there?

Has her job in service of Elwan Bek moved from the villa to the apartment?

Adawi's investigations are unfinished. They must be finished. But why? What exactly is the goal?

He thought to himself as he considered one of two possibilities: either her master had decided to transfer her services to the apartment so that he could use them for other purposes; or he had moved her job there so that he could be alone with her away from his wife and children; or another reason that Adawi couldn't guess.

Who would have taken her place in the villa? The home of the Elwan Bek family?

Adawi spent several days skulking near Elwan's Villa and made some useful observations:

There is another woman working for the family.

The strange thing is that Elwan Bek never spends all day at the villa. although Adawi used to see him there in the past, and he remembers the Bek speaking to him one day in a tone of contempt and disdain.

"Yes, Mr Adawi. Are you coming to assist Sanniya or what?"

Adawi remained silent at the time. He couldn't think of anything to say. He actually came for another reason. He needed a couple of piasters to keep himself high. Is he stupid, or is he out of it on drugs but not to the point of declaring it?

He fell silent and felt an odd desire to vanish completely from the earth's surface. But he was obligated to respond to the villa owner's question, who gave his wife enough money every month and more, for living and getting high too.

"Actually, I'm here for some work, so I said I would look in on her."

On that day, Adawi recalls being unable to be alone with his wife and get what he came for, and then spending a miserable time because he could not get Sanniya's money, with which he could have got enough hash to enjoy all night.

Sanniya surrendered to Elwan. What will you do, Adawi, when she is a capable whore?

You are the cause of all of this. You are the reason. You lost your job and drowned in the drug that exhausts your entire mind. You are the one who was defeated, Adawi, because of your nature. No, your nature is the cause of your destruction. What is left for you to do? And there is no need, because you can't do anything. Even if you consider exacting revenge on her, what will you do? Kill her? So, she'll die, and you'll live. But in prison, and you'll be sentenced to death and die as well. What have we gained?

Let us keep quiet for a long time, working on ourselves, I don't know. We're alive without feeling like we're alive.

Adawi went into a long stretch in which he lost a lot of his sense of many things. He also lost the ability to think clearly, so he decided to stop thinking altogether.

Adawi was in a state where he could not notice the passage of time for a moment, perhaps several hours. As usual, he was talking to himself.

"Man, what if you caught her in Elwan's arms?

"Perhaps the elegant man is trying to wink at you to avoid a scandal.

"It is possible to threaten him to get more from him.

"However, it is also possible that nothing is wrong, and you're just paranoid!

"No no no. It's also possible that Sanniya found her another job in the Elwan Bek building, no big deal.

"Okay, but why is she keeping it from me, Adawi?

"Why did she lose faith in me so quickly, man? What obligates her to tell you?

"And the work?

"Adawi, shut up, before it's too late, shut up. Do not throw away what you have in your hands by performing an insignificant act."

***

When the women of Hanging Bird Lane refer to Sanniya, they call her the mother of seven girls. Everyone, or at least most of them, along with their husbands and children, is aware that Amal is the seventh and final daughter born to the girls' mother. She gave in to the desire of Adawi, the father of the girls. He and the midwife, Sithom, conspired with them to consider, announce, and register Amal as a boy.

Although Sanniya left the lane a long time ago, and some people assumed she would never return, she reappeared once and disappeared several times, and after a long absence, some of her acquaintances suspected she had been divorced.

Others claimed she had vanished from the house she had moved to with Adawi and the remaining girls, and that she had turned to an activity that was nothing to do with her domestic job.

One of the residents said: "I saw her with my own eyes, may I be stricken blind. She got out of a very luxurious Mercedes, which a VIP was driving himself."

THIRD STAGE

How do I escape from this torment?

I'm Hosnia, Amal's friend. I dislike her being in the situation she has been in from her birth until now.

Everyone around her treats her like a boy, but she is a girl. According to her, her father and mother conspired with the midwife to register her as a baby boy in the birth records.

She is a friend of mine from primary school and middle school, and despite being labelled as a boy throughout her school years, she preferred to play with us, her female classmates, over the boys. This used to make me feel astonished, surprised, and reflective. Even though I was young at the time, I noticed she had the features of a girl like us. Her hair is like ours. And that her voice, laughter, shyness, are all girlish, and when I approached her more and revealed some details and secrets about me and my family, she began talking to me freely and boldly when we walked alone on the way to and from school. She claimed she couldn't tell the difference between a girl and a boy. It didn't matter to her whether she was a boy or a girl, or that all her sisters were older than her, making her the last of the girls. They all surround her with love, care, and tenderness, and do not treat her as a boy unless her mother and her father or either of them is around!

They are all aware that she's the seventh girl. And that her parents were adamant about having a son after the six daughters.

One of my memories of Amal is that she often prefers to sit alone. She enjoys solitude and does not speak much unless she is in the middle of a group of us girls with no boys around, and we all—except me—treat her like a boy, something she was not comfortable with, but at the same time, she used to plead with me to keep her secret to myself so that she would not be expelled from school. She occasionally decides to go out with me after school. We meet in private, with no one noticing. She tells me about her daily ordeals, and, being a girl, I tell her about mine as well.

I once asked her, "Why do you complain about being treated like a boy? Isn't it enough that we, as girls, are constantly treated in ways that hurt our feelings? I wish I were a boy, Amal, so I could have what boys have. You know, I think sometimes to myself that, in this life, I have been wronged because I came out as a girl.

"Between you and me, Amal, my dear, I envy that you are a boy. Everyone treats you like a boy. I would never be sad or annoyed by that if I were you. Could I be a boy? I wish we could swap."

We were walking through the crowded streets, and I realized people did not seem to mind that we

were a boy and a girl walking alone, and I wondered
if they thought we were brother and sister. Amal
abruptly came to a halt. Her facial features changed,
as did her stature, and she whispered, "You think it
would be better for me to exploit this situation, drive
in it, and live like a boy, a man?"

Amal seemed troubled, as she does most of the
time, but she was irritable and might be inclined
to consider what I said to her a while ago. It was
extremely challenging for me. I wished I could offer
her some assistance, but what do I have? Nothing.

***

I don't know what I am. A boy, as my father and mother
intended, or a girl, as I feel within myself. I'm always
confused, and sometimes I wonder if being a boy or a
girl is better for me. I'm even more confused than before!
Will my whole life be like this? When I'm around boys,
I feel at ease and whole, speaking, moving, expressing
myself, laughing, screaming, punching, hitting, and
cursing with masculine, boyish rudeness. I have noticed
that the boys I hang out with, whether in the lane, our
lane, Hanging Bird Lane, or at school or in other places
and situations, some of them treat me like a girl, although
everyone around me, except for my Aunt Kamela, treats
me as a boy. They treat me like a boy because my general
appearance has long been controlled by my father and
mother, so I wear boys' clothes and comb my hair like
a boy, and they care a lot about my hair looking like a
boy's hair, but because there are boys around, especially
schoolmates, and because we spend more time together

than we do in the lane or anywhere else, they believe I am not a boy as it appears on the surface. One of them came over to take advantage of an opportunity and placed his hand roughly between my legs. Then, as we were leaving the last class of the day at school, he attacked me in the middle of a group of students and shouted in a scandalous voice, as if he had discovered a new planet that no one else had discovered before him, or as if he had discovered the theories of gravity and buoyancy. He yelled, as if he were Archimedes, "Son of a bitch, always treat yourself as a boy!"

Some of my friends saved me from this terrible situation when I was about ten years old, when some fellow students wrestled with him and thought he was trying to offend me and tarnish my reputation, as he had done in previous situations with other students. He is well-known for his criminal tendencies and attacks on weak students in the class and throughout the school.

I survived, but it was only a matter of days before Qadri struck again. This time, I was alone in a far corner of the school, with no one around me, which happens to me frequently. I'm always avoiding social situations. I'm afraid of being exposed, so I sit quietly by myself and relax a lot. The truth is that Qadri was calm this time and showed no signs of aggression. He greeted me and asked if I needed assistance. And when he found me, I raised both hands defensively to my face as an automatic reaction to my sudden sight of him in this far corner, and I didn't even listen to what he was saying. He laughed aloud and told me while standing still, without moving or approaching,

"Listen, Amal. I know you're a girl, and I know your parents told you that you should be a healthy son. That's awful. How did it happen?

"I didn't mean to bother you on that day. I always pray for you. I can feel something is wrong with you. Of course, I do not know what it is."

I was listening to him even though I didn't want to and was terrified of what was going to happen next. He continued to speak.

"What exactly is your fault? Your parents had daughters, and they yearned for a son. They made you a boy against your will."

"Who told you that?"

"I did ask. People from the lane told me about your story. They are aware but keep quiet."

"Do you take everything you hear seriously?"

"I had a feeling you were a girl, and the things that the people of Hanging Bird Lane told me confirmed my suspicions. Have you forgotten about when our classmates were being weird and surrounded you? I let it go. It was difficult for me. It is true I am mischievous, like the man in *Wesh Egram*, just like what everyone has told you about me. But you were nice to me at the time, and I felt you were a poor guy oppressed by everyone, so I told myself, 'Don't add to her troubles, she has enough as it is'. Listen, Amal, I want to help you, but I don't know what to do."

"How are you going to help me? Do you know how to help yourself, smart guy?"

"What exactly do you mean?"

"Instead of worrying about helping me, leave me alone and focus on yourself."

"When I said I wanted to help you, did I made a mistake? You turned on me straight away.

"I want to help you overcome this condition as well. Our entire class calls you Kedra (Pot). Do you understand why? Because you are lost. You are not aware of yourself or your future."

Qadri found himself on the defensive, though he always actually on the offensive.

He offered to walk her home, and they talked the entire way. Amal welcomed this because she felt that something good was about to appear or happen; somehow Qadri was changing from one state to another.

They walked together and talked as if they were loyal brother and sister. Amal felt at ease and hopeful for some reason, at least for the time being.

★★★

For a long time, she couldn't find anyone to talk to and open her little heart to, except for her aunt, the only man in the family, as she describes her.

Now this Qadri has arrived unexpectedly. Is this Amal's fate?!

He was evil, aggressive, and offensive, attacking all the students and boasting that he was a criminal and that no one could beat him, etc.

But she realized there was something different behind, within this beast. A human in good and chivalrous, with a strong desire to sacrifice for the sake of others, for the sake of Amal.

He told her his story, and everything that had been hidden became clear to her.

"Amal! I must be like you and everyone else who knows me sees me. If I appear to people as a well-disciplined, simple, nice guy, they will eat me up. I know that everyone around me despises me and flees when they see me. And hope that God takes me in the first batch, but what is a difficult life? Even if I pour out kindness, it is difficult in this world – you are either the conquerors or the conquered, and I dislike conquering.

"After my father fled and abandoned us, my mother taught me that strength was more important than truth, and that to survive in this world, everyone must respect and fear you. She was not like that at first, she told me, but the man she married, my father, whom I never knew, turned her inside out, making her fierce and harsh. After he disappeared and left her with children, of which I'm the third, the mother of the men, started buying and selling everything in the market, and she rejected any man after that, saying, 'I am a man, I do not need a man. I am a man's woman'."

***

After the third class, the bell rang, and recess began. We all ran towards the playground; some of us went to the canteen to buy sweets and something to eat, while others preferred to sit in a corner under a lonely tree. I was wondering, am I hungry? Or maybe it's better for me to have some fun with my classmates. Ayesh arrived. He is the oldest of us in school because he was held back several times and had to repeat the school year. He is the leader of a group of students who break all the codes and rules, and once went as far as to lead his small gang in a robbery of the school after the end of the school day, and despite his concealment and complete denial of it, the matter was not kept from the school headmaster. After months and months of enticing the weakest members of the Ayesh El-Beltawi gang with promises of protection and assistance in improving their academic level, etc., Sarhan spoke up and provided accurate information about the operation. He claimed that the incident began as a matter of fun, entertainment, and adventure, but quickly developed into a well-planned scheme and ended up with stealing some equipment, tools, books, and teaching aids.

Ayesh proposed a clever plan to rob the school, and I am not sure why he chose me to be a part of his gang. Is it because I'm a secretive, calm boy, free of suspicions about him? I'm not sure. Is it because I spend most of my recess time secluded in a far corner? He never sought my approval; he simply imposed his decision on me that I would be a gang member. When I tried to avoid the criminal operation, which I would not contemplate and in which I could not participate, he said emphatically, "You are with us, Amal, mate, make no bones about it, because you know the plan. Be a man, show your intelligence, and your share will be safe."

I was threatened by Abu Racine. I discovered I couldn't get away from his influence. I was afraid that he would cause harm to me, and that he and his gang members would abuse me.

Abu Racine, as Ayesh al-Beltawi was known, thought he was smarter than everyone else around him, including students, lackeys, teachers, and even the headmaster. Until such time as he proved his claim to himself and us, he was busy plotting a criminal operation that he did not recognize as such. His intended plan was set down. He relied on his gang's four members: Sarhan, Sa'fan, Sayed Juma'a, and Hassan al-Taher. I had no idea until now what the secret behind adding me to the gang was, which was able first, with his leadership, of course, to overlook one of the couriers in charge of opening the stores – a good, tall, old man. They managed to hide the key from him after they took it from the lockers and distracted him by getting him to break up an improvised brawl between me and one of them, and this was the role assigned to me in the plan.

The rest of the details that I didn't know before were revealed in the morning assembly by the headmaster. I was terrified. Did the school principal know I was a member of the gang? What would happen to me? He had to have known. I'm done. My life ended before it had even started. My failure. I almost peed myself while waiting in line to hear what the headmaster had to say.

Mr Abdul Alim, the school's headmaster, proudly told us, as if he were Salah al-Din, celebrating his victory at the Battle of Jerusalem, that the Abu Racine gang, who stole school supplies and tools worth huge sums, had been exposed. He concluded his lengthy, convulsive speech by stating that he would act in accordance with his conscience on the matter. I recall his words now, but I didn't understand most of them at the time. This heightened my sense of terror.

Following that, we discovered that the headmaster had failed to notify the police or the Directorate of Education, to which our school belonged. We were astonished. We later found out why: the principal was concerned about the future of the young gang members who were his students, and he feared that exposing the matter would lead to the expansion of investigations and the formation of multiple committees by the educational directorate to investigate what had happened, and these committees might want to accuse the school administration, including the principal. The occurrence of such a crime in the school where he is entrusted with its management and safeguarding, as well as, above all, with nurturing and educating its students, means that something had gone wrong with the school administration, and that would be the direct responsibility of the principal. One or all the investigation committees, of which there are usually three, may recommend he be punished, dismissed, or demoted.

The headmaster assured us that he would personally handle the situation to maintain order and preserve the school's dignity and reputation. Following that, when we inquired about the meaning of the headmaster's speech, one of the teachers explained to us that the matter would be closed, it would not go beyond the school gate. This is exactly what happened, and as a result, I survived, and I overcame the state of terror that haunted me for the rest of the time following the headmaster's speech, until we, the students, and everyone in the school, made certain that the headmaster, Abdul Alim, himself, was going to deal with it.

However, the headmaster's silence about the crime, as well as his failure to notify the authorities and the police, was a crime in and of itself. Following that, I noticed that the Abu Racine gang successfully continued its criminal activities both inside and outside of the school. I didn't take part in any of this, and the gang's leader, my fellow veteran student, Ayesh al-Beltawy, didn't hate me for it.

He once told me that I was a failed dude who lacked the talents and abilities required for gang membership and that if he had let me stay with them, I would have exposed them with my stupidity and improvisation. But he threatened me that my life and neck were in his hands, and that he would not let me breathe a single breath if I showed weakness and reported them, as our classmate Serhan Al-Mansi had done... and you know what happened to him. Of course, I was aware that after a while, he was involved in a serious accident and was forced to drop out of school. The gang was said to be behind it.

The last thing Abu Racine said to me was that he had begun to suspect that what some people had said about me was correct: that I am a girl, not a boy!

★★

Abu Racine then attempted to profit from the discovery that I am a girl rather than a boy, as is normal. He started to warm up to me. When he saw me, he gave me a stupid yellow smile, and every now and then, he would surprise me with a piece of candy, an apple, or a fancy pen, and he would react violently if I tried to return anything I found on my desk in the classroom that he had left for me. Once he deliberately came behind me without my knowing and pressed himself to me. Everyone had left the classroom after the last period before recess. He came there on the pretext of giving me a gift. However, he forced me to accept what he had offered me, holding my arm, touching my chest, or even extending his thick fingers to touch between my legs!

Every time I yelled at him, scratched him, tried to bite him, resisted him, and every time he beat me.

He managed to kiss me many times and ran away, and other times he squeezed my breasts, which my family concealed behind baggy clothes, forcing me to drown inside them.

My problem was that I couldn't complain about him because I was afraid the school administration would find out and expel me because my parents forged my official documents and claimed I was a boy.

Abu Racine seemed to be certain that I would not complain to the school administration or anyone else about his harassment, explicit sexual harassment, of me. He did not start anything unless he was sure the coast was clear and that no one could see him.

Now I can admit that after a while of his harassment and molestation, I felt a need for all of it. He is the first person who has made me feel feminine.

He was cheeky and rough, but as a man or young man, years older than me, he made me feel his manhood, and most importantly, he caused my sense of femininity, which my father and mother had purposefully killed and erased, to flourish. It was dormant until Abu Racine dared to provoke it, and while I fiercely resisted him at first, the female instinct that flourished in his hands later became a possession of his.

When I was about twelve, I surrendered to him. I did not submit to Abu Racine, but to the masculine animalism he demonstrated before me. Deep down, despite my hatred for this criminal boy, I was happiest when he hugged me, messed with me, and played games with me like teenagers who know nothing of the art of intimate relationships.

He is, of course, ignorant of sexual matters, which was to my advantage because it made him unconcerned about my virginity. So, despite his pursuit, harassment, and intrusion into my innocence, I remained a virgin. He would drag me to deserted places inside and outside the school, and I pretended to resist, but with that, I surrendered to his urgency, I celebrated the exciting clandestine meeting, and I showed him some kind of objection, but with time and repetition, and my longing and even eagerness for Abu Racine to do what he was doing with me, my claims of reluctance collapsed, and he felt it and no longer compelled me to accompany him to the place which he had chosen for our intimate practices. He would simply point at it, or he would whisper the name of the place or the secluded corner that would witness our secret adventure in a few moments.

Meanwhile, a significant development occurred. The features of my femininity became more and more visible, and my family made more of an effort to conceal them by cutting my hair, making me wear loose clothing. I'm not sure where my father got the idea for me to drink vinegar more than once a day until I shrunk, and so that the features of my femininity, the chest and buttocks, and the voice, couldn't crystalize.

But my frantic efforts to remain a boy were futile and it seemed that my situation would be revealed at some point.

My mother was unconcerned by any of this. My father was so worried and upset that they forced me to drop out of school so that their secret would not be revealed and they would not be subjected to problems and court action that could lead to dire consequences and to his imprisonment on charges of forgery of official papers and data.

I felt forced to leave school. If it had been up to me, I would have stayed, if possible, just like our other long-time student, Abu Racine (who ended our relationship after I stopped going to school).

My school life was full of fears, problems, and crimes, but it was also full of life.

My father forced me to leave school. His argument was that he could no longer afford the cost of that corral, which he called 'Sanniya's burden', as a form of punishment for my mother because of her daughters. Of course, that was not the reason. It was simply a strong and logical argument.

The actual reason is both known and unknown!

No one says it openly, not even ambiguously, as a known reason, and everyone claims it's unknown, nameless, and they insist on publicly repeating my father's argument: it's his right as a loving parent.

And, submissively and affectionately, my mother told my father, Amal is the only boy, and he will be able to find a job and help with household expenses. The family has no means of support. Your father isn't always able to earn a living. We would have died of hunger if God had not blessed me with my job."

I am vehemently opposed, saying, "The girls are all working somewhere. The food is plentiful. Why don't you take me out of school? It is even possible for an educated person to find a better job than a dropout?"

Realizing she is deceiving and lying, she says, "Will you, barely out of nappies, teach us what is best, what is most appropriate?"

I exclaim and yell, "Also, you treated me like a boy and forgot the truth. Why deprive me of the creation of the Lord, who begat me on earth, just because I am Amal, your last daughter? This is defamation. God will exact vengeance on you for all of this. I will not sit here for it for even for a second."

★★★

Her father forced her to drop out of school and work in menial jobs as a boy.

A coffee boy, a shoe shiner, a beggar at a nearby hospital.

These were jobs Adawi had which he used to take Amal to, and because he couldn't hold down a job, he returned to his previous state, which he seemed to prefer and enjoy now: unemployed!

Although his neighbours in the lane that he moved to shortly after Al-Haja Kamela's headbutt were following the stories and tales of his failure and expulsion from every job he had, they noticed that even when he was expelled from a job, in a cafe, with a contractor, or in a store, he would work it for a short while before quitting, and they knew the secret was Sanniya. Had it not been for her stable occupation in people's homes and her recent stable job in the service of the family of Elwan al-Malwani, a well-known businessman, Adawi lived his long days and nights as if he were jobless thanks to an inheritance. His wife's livelihood was more than sufficient.

And why looking for work in the first place? Where can he look for work? And why is he not content with his exquisite state? Professional Status: Unemployed!

***

After I began polishing his right shoe, the customer yelled at me. He was sitting on the roadside in a local cheap café, which was not frequented by respectable people like him. I had no clue why he had come to that place. His appearance suggested that he had a reasonable occupation. He was clad in posh clothes, not those of simple workers or even traders. He left for me the task of polishing his shoes, and ran off with the newspaper, which he read with strange interest. My client's age was twice my age, or so it seemed, and he was looking at me suspiciously, or so it seemed. My appearance was unusual, that is true, but I did not expect anyone would be suspicious. Although I was dressed in a peasant kaftan and a turban, and I had concealed the outlines of my chest with padding that my mother had placed under the kaftan with a hidden nightgown over it. Of course, my face was on display, and there was no hiding the softness of my skin or the tenderness of my voice. Even my attempts to deepen my voice, as my father urged me to do, appeared feeble.

I walked away with a layer of polish on the right shoe, sitting on a small wooden chair that I always kept with me.

I'm not sure why, but I imagined myself in the shoes of this customer, and I wondered how I could be like him!

I was struck by his stature, masculinity, and respectable demeanour ever since he asked for his boots shined in a commanding voice, as if he would kindly favour me with a few pennies to keep me from being lost.

Suddenly, the customer erupted, yelling, "You're such a twit! What are you, an idiot? What's with the brown paint on black boots?"

The ground fell out from beneath my feet, and I was overcome with fear. What is this man going to do to me? What will my father say when he learns what happened? Thank God, he's not sitting next to me like he usually does since we've been coming to the market together. He had gone in search of his high.

"Sorry, sir, I got lost in the treachery of time and wandered far from you, but I will fix the mistake right away in the blink of an eye, and everything will be perfect."

It was a difficult task, and my father had vanished, and I wished he could have saved me, but the man was tolerant after his outburst of rage. Perhaps my enticing words had softened his heart toward me.

He muttered incomprehensible words and waved his hand, as if daring me to back up my claims.

He went back to his newspaper, sinking between its lines and pages once more.

I'm not sure how God gave me the ability to escape this situation that I unintentionally put myself in, even though it took time. I had to remove all traces of the brown colour and use a black lacquer lotion to prepare the leather of the right shoe. I let it rest on the clean leather before covering it with a second, more abundant sponging. I then let it rest. My struggle to restore the right shoe to its natural colour was successful and finished. My job was done, and I called to my client with the glee of a survivor, telling him that he'd never seen his shoes as good as they are now!

"Magnificent."

He was satisfied with one word and stood looking at the shoes again from a different angle. Then I found him stroking my cheek with his hand and giving me twice as much as I had asked for as payment. He left his café seat in a graceful way, blinking at his shiny shoes repeatedly.

I noticed a brighter gleam on his face.

***

The neighbourhood is opulent, the residents are sophisticated, and the job that my father has placed me in is his old trade: an ironing boy.

He was not working with me this time, so he delegated my duties to one of his old colleagues. Al-Usta Alata is his name. He was working in his shop and was one of the boys of his father, al-Haj Samahi. Alata was not his name, of course. His name was Shaban, but he was known for his prestige and bragging about his perfection at his craft. Some customers even demanded that only Alata and not any other boy iron their clothes. That was the story told to me by my father on the way to the upper-class ironing shop. He didn't forget to tell me how much he envied the al-Wad Alata because my grandfather relied on him, trusted him, and preferred him over his only son, Adawi.

I was wondering how Alata became the owner of a shop in an upscale neighbourhood while being nothing more than an ironing boy, or even an ironing man, while my father, who inherited his father's shop, failed to manage it, went bankrupt, and closed the shop because of the debt he had accumulated.

I didn't ask my father at the time, but I later learned that the reason was obvious and needed no explanation, because Shaban took the matter seriously (as my mother told me), whereas my father lived on his father's back and did not take any issue seriously, as you can see.

I cannot deny that al-Usta Alata was both chivalrous and honest with me. He did not exhaust me at work. He accepted me only because I reminded him of my grandfather and his favours to him, and because he would not refuse any of father's requests, although he did not need me or anyone else, and his three boys were doing a good job.

Alata didn't notice I wasn't a boy. And he was always busy reliving some of his memories of working with my grandfather with me whenever he had the chance. And, in honour of this memory, he did not assign me any arduous tasks, and it was as if unemployed. I had no job other than to go to the market and buy what he needed or to deliver some ironing to its owners' homes. He ended up leaving me free for the task of delivering the ironing to the customers. He said that I had a beautiful smile and a cheerful face, and he brought me elegant clothes with the shop logo on them. He stated he would be the first ironer in Egypt to offer a home delivery service, and that he might consider expanding the process to include receiving the ironing from the customers' homes. The customer just had to phone the store.

I like this guy. He enjoys his work and is proud of it. He excels and grows in it. And, of course, I noticed he has a good reputation; I knew he did not smoke, drink alcohol, or use drugs; I noticed that he did not utter obscene words, and also that he was well-liked by customers and shop owners.

But, despite all Al-Usta Alata's good qualities and the care that he surrounded me, I quit working for him.

He sent me with ironed clothes to deliver them to a customer.

I was surprised to see the man wearing his underwear when he opened the door to his apartment for me to pick up his shirts and clothes. He was a retired man taken aback by me and quickly left me inside the apartment, closing the door. An apartment that looked like a palace that I had only seen on TV, window coverings, impressive furnishings, beautiful decor, a delicious breeze, and a calm that was both relaxing and frightening.

The man returned, wearing a silk robe and holding a sum of money. He approached me with an expression of regret on his face. He placed the money on a nearby table and extended his arms to take the ironed clothes from me. His hand landed on my chest by accident. And it was by chance that this man discovered that I was not a boy because he and all the customers and everyone here treated me like a boy. All his facial expressions bore shock, surprise, questions, and, of course, exclamation.

I bent over and took his hands in mine, swearing and begging him not to tell anyone about my secret so that my life would not be cut short.

He listened to me quietly and patiently. I kept talking. He continued to listen, showing no signs of emotion in his features. He was speaking to himself in hushed tones.

When I finished speaking, he was sitting on a luxurious sofa in front of me, and he invited me to sit next to him, and told me that my secret would be kept safe, that he admired my courage and knew the hardships of life. As he continued to speak, he rose to go to the kitchen while saying, "life is difficult, Amal".

I was terrified. I'm not sure how to put it. What was this man going to do to me? Why did he walk into the kitchen unexpectedly? Why did he open the door for me while he was still in his underwear? And did he purposefully touch my chest while he took his clothes from me?

I was surrounded by questions and terrified of this man's calmness when I found him returning from the kitchen with a knife in his hand!

In the blink of an eye, I jumped from the sofa where I was sitting and was at the door. But he caught up with me and shut the door as the knife fell from his grasp, so I threw myself on the knife. I took hold of it and pointed it in his face, so he gave me his other hand, holding an apple!

"Don't be afraid, Amal. Don't be afraid of me. I brought you an apple."

I'm not sure what I was feeling at the time, somewhere between horror and joy. I relaxed a little and took the apple from his hand, gesturing to him to apologize for my fears and doubts. He left me, went to the kitchen again, and returned with a glass of water and a second apple. He smiled as he handed me the water.

"Listen, Amal. I will certainly keep your secret, but I have a simple request. First, drink water to relax, and eat this delicious apple, and I will pay your fare and add some more for you, but I want you to show me this hidden beauty. I will just watch, without touching or doing anything. What do you say?"

I refused vehemently and threw the apple away, so he came up behind me and grabbed my chest and squeezed it with both hands, saying, "you either show me, or I expose you?"

At this point his entire appearance and demeanour had, in my eyes, transformed into a demon's!

I'm a prisoner in a cramped apartment with a strange man. He has in his hands both the key and my secret. He can expose me.

I begged him to spare me and leave me alone. I told him that I was running late for work, but he ignored me. He was busy unbuttoning my jacket and removing the stuffing I was using to conceal the protrusion of my chest, and I was like a slaughtered chicken, stubborn while slaughtered!

This pig was not only staring at my protruding breasts, but he stripped me off completely and was enjoying his eyes staring and his hands touching everything; I felt like nothing.

When I returned to the shop, I informed Al-Usta Alata that I was tired and had nearly passed out, which caused the delay. He agreed to let me leave work immediately and go home because I appeared pale and ill.

I never returned to the upper-class ironing shop after that.

My father listened to my story about the old customer, and I decided I would not continue this work.

He knew I was unfit for the jobs he forced me to do, but he aimed to keep me out of any situation in which my secret would be exposed, so that everyone would know that I am a girl, not a boy, as he claims. Despite my young age at the time, this was not far from my mind. At first, I could not figure out anything and became confused, so I assumed that my work with him was of some help, but it soon became clear that he was not working. He simply immerses me in my job and its circumstances, drowning me in the minutiae, so that everyone knows I was born as a boy as he rumoured. Why am I the only girl whose mother did not take me to work as a housecleaner like her and all six of my sisters?

I only found one explanation: my father and mother, of course, wanted to prove that I was a boy.

How can I get out of this torment?

I kept thinking and searching for a way to end this agony. I'm about 18 years old, and despite their best efforts to erase my femininity, it is visible, and yet they foist on me the clothes and appearance of a boy.

I decided to flee from it all.

FOURTH STAGE

Inshirah is the Answer!

If I had known what was going to happen to me all those years ago, I would not have stayed on the planet for a single second.

But all my attempts to end this torment were futile.

The first time I thought I'd be saved from my torment was when I was able to flee from my family. To where? I'm not sure, and it doesn't matter. Which places and people in the world would be better and more merciful? I said, oh girl, your real chance is to die quickly in any way. But what is the way, and which way is it?

I'm not sure. I heard about a girl from Hanging Bird Lane. Her family allegedly caught her with a boy and locked her in the house, so she committed suicide. But her family caught her. I'll try to recall how she attempted to do it. My sister, Atta, reminded me of her. She informed me that she was a classmate of mine at school and told me the story with passion.

She made me swear not to think of attempting suicide like Inshirah.

What exactly did she say?

She said that she was working as a nurse in a dispensary and took the right amount of poison, swallowing it.

And where would I get the poison? I pondered and rummaged through my memories.

Ah, I've found it!

***

After a while, Amal was able to contact Inshirah, an old classmate who had consoled her when she realized she was not a boy as they had imposed on her, and from time to time she shared stories about the suffering of girls with her.

Inshirah is the answer!

It was not easy to get to the Wellness Clinic. Amal suffered along the journey, which included questioning, disorientation, and harassment, and she was given the wrong directions several times. Some of the people she asked pointed her to places, neighbourhoods, areas, and addresses that didn't even have a clinic in them.

One of them, a man in his fifties who appeared withdrawn, took her to a deserted location and attempted to rape her (he tried to rape her because she looked like a little boy). And when he dared to forcefully strip his prey, he discovered it was a girl! A girl's screams and groans, and he (the aggressor) isn't interested in little girls: boys or nothing.

The man's preference for boys saved her from a certain rape case.

This was one of the few times Amal escaped simply because she was female.

Another time, and possibly a third, after losing hope of finding a wellness clinic, she began to look for the house where Inshirah was hiding and, after a long struggle, she managed to find the house, but she did not find Inshirah there. Everyone she asked about her told her that she was occasionally late for work, and an elderly woman sitting on the stairs asked, "If you need medical attention, my son, why don't you go to the clinic?"

She showed her the way, and Amal was relieved to find out where the Clinic was because her trip there would be all the more pleasant, at least until she bought the poisons she required, at which point everything would be over.

Another day, she was there. Inshirah remembered her and greeted her warmly, and when Amal found a moment to explain what she needed from her, her former classmate, who was famous for her failed suicide attempt, was stunned. She took her into a room in the clinic away from the patients, doctors and nurses and began a lengthy discourse about what had happened to her after she miraculously escaped death while attempting to escape her life of torment following her scandal.

"Amal, suicide is not the solution. The world is vast, very vast, and not everyone is against you. The future is in your hands. It's foolish to close your eyes to that. What's the point if everyone commits suicide when they run into a problem like this?

"If that were the case, the entire world would have committed suicide because of their problems. What I learned and the good people around me taught me that the world doesn't have just one barrier and if it's closed, you're out of luck; no, Amal, the world doesn't have barriers, it's infinite.

"Hope and determination are more important than despair and suicide. How can you bear the name Amal (Hope) while contemplating suicide?!

"If I were you, I would look for work in a faraway place, away from everyone who wants you to be a boy." She fell silent abruptly, as if an idea had struck her, then she exclaimed, "Why don't you come to live with me, and I will find you work, and you can cut off your family for good?"

Amal sat quietly listening and turning her thoughts around, trying to find the reason in Inshirah's words. The words shocked her at first because she had struggled to get here and her entire body had been made ready for only one idea: suicide, salvation from everything she has to go through every moment of every day. Her former classmate was now asking her to drop the idea entirely.

Amal lost her ability to think clearly. Her mental, spiritual, and psychological energy faded under the time, suffering, and the siege where she felt she was the hanging bird rather than her lane. The Hanging Bird. It didn't fly and soar, nor did it fall, and it was over.

It has to be over. (She whispered to herself.)

Inshirah sensed that her old classmate was troubled by thoughts and emotions, so she invited her back and promised her that a little rest and relaxation, a good drink, and a delicious meal would help make her feel comfortable and happy.

Amal responded completely surrendered, as if she had given up control over the matter and taken a path over which she had no say.

The lane in which Inshirah lives is not dissimilar to Hanging Bird Lane. and Amal drifts unconsciously and without regard for the consequences. She believes that something must occur. She has an inner feeling, which she cannot explain, that her life will never be the same again, but she is unsure whether what is to come will be better or worse!

She tells herself that whatever happens to her will not be worse than the death she had been yearning for recently and which she was deprived of by Inshirah with the power of her words and experience.

She lets events take their course, whatever will be will be.

She enters the house with Inshirah, climbs the stairs, sighs, and takes a deep breath in search of a breath of air to inhale before her breath stops.

The apartment she entered behind her old classmate made her catch her breath. Mess, carpets, dishes in a sink waiting for someone to wash them, laundry spread over the edges of the chairs, underwear strewn about, there was a small TV facing you with a sofa opposite it. She and her classmate sat on it to take a breather.

"Sorry the apartment is a mess. I wasn't expecting that anyone would visit."

Inshirah quickly gathers items, piles them in corners, and arranges other things. She suddenly begins to take off her clothes, item by item.

Then, she asks Amal to do the same: "Let yourself go, honey, relax."

She walks to the bathroom while Amal timidly begins to remove the boy's clothes that she had been made to wear, but keeps her underwear on.

Her colleague returned, freshly showered, and dressed in a transparent nightgown, and directed her to the bathroom.

When she came out, having washed herself, she discovered a nightgown given to her by Inshirah, and she exclaimed, "You're from now a girl!"

There was a copper tray with food on the floor, and the voice of Umm Kulthum echoing from a transistor that was barely visible.

Inshirah told her entire story while they were eating and relaxing on the floor.

Amal learned that her former colleague had fled her family after her scandal and failed suicide attempt. She moved from job to job and residence to residence, and as time passed, she lost her desire for men. She preferred a celibate life.

She promised Amal she would help her find work. She promised her that her life would improve. She told her she shouldn't be afraid of anything.

But Amal was terrified, with a vague feeling that something was going to happen.

Nothing happened.

Amal appeared calm and tranquil in Inshirah's apartment, but anxiety rattled its sabres.

The classmate left her to rest on the first day, and went to work. Amal found herself doing nothing but cleaning and organizing the apartment in an attempt to escape the turmoil into which she was falling, despite the feelings of relief she was experiencing as she spent her first days as a female!

Inshirah's story was painful, as she had fallen in love with a boy from her neighbourhood when she was in her early adolescence and sank into a secret relationship with him until she surrendered herself to him out of love, longing, adventure, and going all in. Her affair with him, however, was exposed when her family caught her in his arms. They made the decision to take everything away from her. They kept her imprisoned in the house. Inshirah lost her awareness and her will to live. She took her own life. Her attempt failed, possibly because she still had the remnants of a desire to stay, perhaps because of her ignorance of the method she used to try to end her life. Of course, it could have been due to her father's coincidental presence and his saving her. After her father died, Inshirah fled her family. She started working as a nurse in another clinic, and her family didn't know how to get there. This is the clinic where she's been working for years.

Inshirah told her old classmate, Amal, who was now her roommate, everything about her past life, even going so far as to say she had no idea what had happened to her that had caused her to lose her inclination for men.

Amal assumed that her stay with Inshirah would be only temporary. She had no idea where she was going to happen next. The most important aspect of her life right now is that she lives as a girl, not a boy!

She was first concerned with finding work, and then there would be a thousand solutions to her problems.

***

It was not long before Inshirah found a job at another clinic for her classmate Amal.

And so, her days go by, boring, empty, and meaningless. A life she leads like cattle. She gets up to go to work and spends the majority of the day, sometimes working for longer hours than her usual daily shift, just to avoid spending the time thinking about herself, her soul, her circumstances, and her future. She immerses herself in her work to the point where she cannot see herself. She runs away from herself, cancels herself, and disintegrates herself.

When she returns in the evening, she is exhausted and unable to enjoy the rest of the long day. She eats and sleeps. Inshirah was frequently found sleeping. She takes a look at her before crawling into bed.

Amal cast her usual look at Inshirah on one occasion, and she was caught between wakefulness and drowsiness. Inshirah smiled at her and made room on one side of the bed for her. It was only a matter of seconds before Amal found herself in her arms. They began by exchanging hot hugs. They drew it out after that. When Inshirah placed her hands on her partner's chest, the hug transformed into a hot, inflamed, and burning physical encounter, an encounter of deprivation, loss, psychological distress, and hunger for the other.

She can't remember when she decided to be a boy, as forced by her parents, and as was stated in her identity card and school papers. Did that incident happen when she was looking for work? Or when her father was working with her? Or now while she is living with her former classmate Inshirah?!

***

I've spent a long time believing that I am distinct from the rest of God's creation. Am I a girl? As far as I know, I am female; I feel and perceive all those sorts of words, or not? I mean, neither a girl nor anything else, a boy, a man. Am I a man?

And if I were a man, why have I lived to this age without having any inclination for any girl, female?

Is it as if I were a man sleeping with other men?

Am I a third type? Neither a man nor a woman?! In between?! I sometimes ask myself, when I feel the effects of the blockade around me, "girl, would it be so bad to be a boy?" Some of my friends and relatives, men, and women, particularly my friend Husnia, who seriously tried to tell me that I am fortunate because my family treats me like a boy, say it would be better.

During an intense argument with me, she once said to me: "If only what happened to you could happen to me. Are you really that horrible? Imagine the difference in our society between a boy and a girl: the scorn, belittlement, and, in some cases, humiliation heaped on all women."

Sometimes, Husnia tells her, she imagines and wishes she were a boy. "Our country's boys are not held accountable, monitored, or punished, nobody hurts their feelings, no one complicates their lives or future. Boys come and go as they please, they do their work however they want. Nobody holds them responsible; on the contrary, their family is proud of him, even if they find out, for example, he knocked up a girl, or got addicted to drugs, or smoking, they will grumble and object in public, but in private, they will say: 'our son is now a man!'.

"Have you ever noticed how the boys are masters of their domain at home? Why don't you thank your Lord that you're a boy, Amal?"

I was struck by a state of disorder, rupture, and a sense of loss of identity and meaning. A sense of despair and distress at life and existence and an old desire to give up my existence and be rid of my life and torments returned to me strongly.

"Is that me?!"

"Am I a man?! … a woman?

Is it possible that I was looking for my femininity in my relationship with Inshirah? Was she arousing, igniting, and feeding feelings and instincts that were suffocating me and holding me against my will? Or was she searching for the man she had lost, the man whom her family had forbidden her from seeing and had caused her torment?

I'm not sure, but there was a pathological state of loss, deprivation, lust, fear, and flight. All of this combined to throw me into a miserable whirlpool, an abnormal, unnatural, inhuman, and useless relationship; a relationship in which neither of us achieves any real satisfaction, recovery, or refreshment, or euphoria or sense of perfection, which I learnt from my readings that women feel in their intimate relationship with men, and men feel with women.

FIFTH STAGE

They All Colluded Against Me.

I only had one place in front of me. It was my aunt Kamela's house.

I had my doubts because it was on the same Hanging Bird Lane, at the end by the north side. Would my parents notice I ran away and took refuge in it?

I came to a halt on the road and thought to myself, "You prat, aren't they going to come and force Kamela to give me back?"

How will Kamela react when I tell her I can't live without her and that I want to live in her care, away from my father and mother, who have it in for me?

Do you think she will send me back and advise me to return to my family's house? She will proclaim to me she cannot snatch me from them like this, and that her defence of me and demand that her sister, my mother, and her husband, my father, treat me as God created me, does not imply attacking her sister's, my mother's, family and depriving her of me.

If that happens, I'll have no choice other than committing suicide. I have no other way out.

I had a cowardly idea when I was a few steps away from Kamela's house. "Return, Amal. There is no hope."

The stupid idea, however, flew away. I found Mama Kamela pleased with my arrival and even more pleased with my decision to flee the captivity of these 'zombies', as she referred to them.

My aunt felt overjoyed at my presence and my request to stay with her and protect me from my father and mother.

She explained to her daughter, Naima, that she didn't want anyone to know that I was here.

She reiterated that my presence there was a secret, and all, including her grandchildren, Naima's children, must keep it secret. That is, Naima must either keep the news of my stay with my aunt Kamela from her children or suggest to any of them who saw me I was just visiting for a short while.

Kamela's thoughts and feelings were troubling her. She was taken aback by Amal's presence. She didn't feel prepared to bear the consequences, not because of any weakness, perhaps because she wished Adawi and Sanniya would give up on their plan to torture Amal by dressing her up as a character that didn't exist. She believed that by defying them, she would be able to prevent them from the evil that had taken them captive. She wanted to give Amal back the existence she had been stripped of and for her to return home as a girl amongst her sister's daughters.

Kamela hadn't wanted the challenge and strife to reach a point where Amal's adventure would end up with her asking for refuge here.

What is Adawi's plan? What is Sanniya's reaction going to be? Will they become even more ferocious than they were with their daughter, Amal?

Kamela cannot respond by returning Amal to her home, to withdraw and apologize for her inability to keep up with her, or to respond to her desire to live a normal life, which her parents deny her, as a female, a girl, a girl with an existence, characteristics, and rights.

Her reasoning settled on the fact that her duty and love for Amal demanded that she open her heart, arms, and home, come what may.

When she realized this, she told her daughter, Naima, to spread the word about Amal's reappearance after her disappearance, her escape from her family's home and her refuge in her aunt's home, with the goal of indirectly informing Adawi and Sanniya.

With this challenge, Kamela's testosterone was rising and activating, and her emotions were regaining vigour and vitality. She even felt the emotions of a mother who is not afraid to give her life for her child.

There was a state of confusion in Al-Haja Kamela's house for several days, which began the moment Amal stepped a foot in it. A discussion, more of a rebuke, took place between Kamela and Amal, as Al-Haja was shocked that Amal had not come to her when she fled her family home. She was also angry with her because she had not informed her of her plans to escape to Inshirah's place.

Amal revealed to her aunt that she hadn't wanted to stay with her old classmate and that she had gone to her to seek her assistance in committing suicide!

The reproach and revelation ended and Kamela determined that Amal must swear to her by God that she had erased her plan to commit suicide from her mind, because "suicide", as Kamela intoned, "is disbelief in God, and you are my daughter, and praise be to God, you are not a disbeliever".

***

Amal now lives with her Aunt Kamela, the family's oldest member, and enjoys being treated like a girl by her aunt. She enjoys spending time with her. Her aunt tries to make up for the suffering, torment, insults, soul sabotage, and distortion experienced by the youngest of the family, Amal, in her parents' house. And she combs her hair and nourishes it with natural ointments and oils. She wraps her like a little bride in the most beautiful, simple, elegant clothes, and offers her the jewels of advice and the juice of her experience with life and people.

Amal is engulfed in feelings of bliss, tranquillity, and rehabilitation of her soul.

In the afternoon, Amal sat and listened to Mama Kamela who gave her a summary of her life experiences. Kamela's speech was not intended for this moment but, speaking with Amal led her to say what she said, fluently and calmly. The degree of spontaneity occasionally surprised Amal, as her old aunt approached sensitive matters.

She was 18 years old, mostly shy, and timid. When she spoke of some matters, she found herself almost hiding her face in her hands, her brown face turning pink and then a fiery red.

Although Amal had heard similar words from girls and boys, in the family, at school, and in the lane, what Al-Haja Kamela told her was different: clear, open, fluent, steady and based on experience, rather than gossip from children, "tykes", as Kamela called them. The talk continued despite the expressions of shyness on her niece's face and the confusion and tension that made the limbs of her fresh body shake.

Kamela reiterated that what she was saying now would benefit Amal for the rest of her life; It would open the pages of the book of the world for her, allowing her to see herself with wide-open eyes rather than with the disappointment that today's girls are experiencing because of their ignorance of life's facts.

Amal, on the other hand, was attempting to maintain her self-control and rise to the level of conversation, and see it as receiving knowledge or science, just like at school during the science and biology classes.

But how can a teen girl surrounded by the circumstances of life, society, and endless pressures be cold while receiving an open explanation of issues relating to the activities and functions of her organs, especially when it works in response and harmony with the organs of another human being, a young teen male like her?

Mama Kamela revealed to her the secrets of taking care of her body and keeping it clean, beautiful, healthy, and well, organ by organ, from the hair on her head to the tips of her toes, and everything in between.

No one will teach her what she is teaching her now, she said.

She explained to her why she believed women were the foundation of everything, it's why women are regarded as a symbol of honour and virtue, and as preservers and protectors of the human race, and it's why they are entrusted with the monumental tasks such as looking after men and caring for children until they mature into men and women.

She explained to her the importance of a woman's self-preservation and concern for the purity of her soul and body.

Amal can't believe what she's hearing. Mama Kamela took her to the bathroom, where she bathed her while continuing to explain.

Amal's shyness faded after a while, replaced by feelings of brilliance, pride, and transcendence she had never experienced in her 18 years of life.

She was in such a state of turmoil three or four years ago that she almost stopped feeling like she was a girl!

Until Kamela rescued her and gradually returned her to her repressed femininity. Right now, she's filled with the sublime sensation of being a girl, a female!

Amal wanders off, and her thoughts lead her into a realm of ambiguous questions. How does Mama Kamela get all this information and knowledge that even university students are unaware of?

Al-Haja Kamela. How does she know all this even though she did not get a very high level of education?

She remained silent for a while.

She reminds herself that knowledge isn't limited to books. Al-Haja Kamela is proof that life is a great school.

Amal laughs loudly, which draws Kamela's attention. She enquires: "What's that for?"

Amal was taken aback. She stammered for a moment before saying, "Something that never occurred to me before, a lovely thought."

"Good. May God bless you."

"I had a dream that I was riding a white horse behind a knight wearing white!"

Amal let out a loud laugh to hide her embarrassment, then leaped to her feet and dashed to the kitchen, proclaiming, "Will you drink tea now, Mama?"

She was having a good time while making tea, and she was thinking about how to interpret her lovely dream, and realized that Haja Kamela knew how to interpret dreams, so she smiled and said, "I have an idea!"

She looked straight into Kamela's eyes as she served tea and poured it into her cup, then whispered: "Mama Kamela, do you want to know the dream I told you about?"

From the first moment Amal recounted what she saw in her dream, Kamela knew and interpreted to herself the meaning of that dream, but she turned the idea in her head and did not comment or explain its meaning or significance. She thought that Amal was attempting to fulfil the image of a woman, which her father had suppressed. Her father and mother assumed she was looking forward to living her life as a woman and that she had reached puberty. She fantasized about a knight on a white horse who would come to her rescue and make her happy. But who would be the right knight for an 18-year-old girl who wore boy's clothes and had a male figure? During those years, she must have been torn emotionally and psychologically, and she must have gained some masculinity from her interactions with young men at school, on the street, and even in the homes of her relatives.

The girl who has regained her femininity. She is looking forward to the beautiful days ahead and the happiness that has manifested itself in the house of Kamela in the Hanging Bird Lane, but what happiness and what future if she is deprived of continuing her education?!

Amal complained to her aunt about the situation. Haja Kamela was her saviour, so Al-Haja pressed her thick, flabby lips together and said, after a moment of thought and consideration:

"Don't worry, my love; education will be paid for by me and will be provided by the best teachers, right here in the family home."

Kamela has found a job for Amal that will pay her a decent wage and allow her to reclaim her femininity and personality that she has been deprived of for so long. An acquaintance, an old friend of her late husband, owns a clothing factory in Ghoria where an army of women and girls work. When Kamela came to him to ask for a job, he was very welcoming.

The job that Ahmed Hamida, the proprietor of the well-known veil-clothing store chain, *Nawara*, procured for Amal was not the job she aspired to, but she didn't turn it down because it was at least a steppingstone.

The man is a well-known businessman with a good reputation who employs a group of girls and women, as well as men and boys, but the prevalent feature among all the employees is what they refer to as commitment. Amal had heard this word used several times to describe someone who lives and acts under the principles of Islam, but who said that she could be described in this way? Amal has not made a commitment. Is it true that Haja Kamela told Ahmed Hamida that she was committed? What if he found out the truth? Would he fire her from the job because she lied? Or maybe he was sceptical of the situation and that's why he put her in a lower position.

Amal was particularly concerned, and she did not feel the relief she had expected to feel after getting a job, rather than being an unemployed woman, thanks to Mama Kamela. Was it because she found herself in a place where all men and women work while praying and muttering Islamic religious verses and expressions from time to time? Or because the girls and women wore long, modest clothes that cover the entire body amply? They are loose baggy clothes, as if they were embroidered sacks. Amal recalled her past. How she was forced to be a boy in her family's house, and the baggy clothes that they made her wear. But they—her father and mother—didn't make her wear a veil, of course, because they treated her like a boy.

In the veil clothing store where Ahmed Hamida assigned her the job in response to Al-Haja Kamela's wishes, she had no specific job. She was to be present every day and wait for the store manager's instructions.

She was introduced to Sister Saleha, the manager, on the first day when Kamela brought her there, as a tough-looking woman with a frightening smile who acted and spoke as if she were a camp leader, not a fashion store manager.

Some of the female workers she encountered told her that the word Saleha connotes a masculinity that is greater than the businessman who owns these stores. Amal did not know what Ahmed Hamida, Brother Hamida, as everyone who worked there called him, from Saleha to the youngest woman, looked like; since he had not been present on the day she arrived and had not appeared since, despite the fact she had been in the shop for more than ten days.

If someone asked Amal what her job was, she wouldn't be able to give them a clear answer because she didn't know the answer to such a question herself!

She arrives early in the morning, but Saleha does not arrive for several hours and none of the director's male or female assistants have any authority. No one directs her to a specific task or job. She asks an assistant what job she was supposed to do. The assistant advises her to wait until Madam Saleha comes and gives her orders.

When Amal hears the phrase Sister Saleha, she goes into a strange state. She secretly thinks to herself, they had better say Mr Saleha, because she is a man disguised in the persona and appearance of a woman.

She just has to wait patiently and in boredom, without work or even the chance to speak with any of the male or female employees. No one has time to gossip because everyone is working.

When the sister arrives, she immediately begins an inspection tour of the premises, hurling orders, notes, and hidden insults everywhere, and Amal tries to find a moment amid all of it to inquire about what she should do today, but she cannot do so because the sister is busy. She does not listen to Amal or anyone else. She questions, holds people accountable, scorns, and dismisses them. She utters lots of religious expressions, such as 'work is worship' and 'believers take responsibility' and 'work is a commitment' and 'God's eyes are on you'. 'Where will you go from the reckoning on the Day of Judgement, misguiding ones?!'

She says it colloquially and emotionally, making Amal afraid that Saleha will be harmed.

Days passed with her not knowing what she was supposed to do there. Everyone was focused on their work, and no one asked, as she did, "What should I do here?"

It is one of a large chain of stores owned by Brother Hamida that specializes in selling fine clothing; this chain also has workshops and factories that produce these fashions, and the company has designers who design everything, including not only dresses, kaftans, jilbabs, hijabs, and other accessories, but also shoes, underwear, handkerchiefs, and a plethora of bonnets, hats, burqas, and gloves. A vast universe in which

Amal is lost.

In fact, she does not agree with this type of environment or attire.

But it's work, and you don't have to like or accept everything. It is, after all, work. What kind of job do you have? What am I supposed to be doing here? No one asks me to do any work, and even the director doesn't seem to have anything on her mind, doesn't ask me what I'm doing, and doesn't tell me what to do!

All of this got to me. I told Mama Kamela and expressed my dissatisfaction.

"Be patient, Amal," she advised. "Our Lord created the world in six days."

"True," I said, "but I've been bored for ten days!"

"Thank God you have a job and a pay cheque to look forward to at the end of the month. Thousands and thousands of people, both men and women, including young men and women, would rather be in your shoes."

***

Amal finished school remotely and was getting ready to tell Mama Kamela that she wanted to look for a different job as a high school graduate employee to help with Kamela's increased expenses. She wishes to repay some of her kindness. She knew Kamela would be adamantly opposed to the idea from the start, and that she would be determined for Amal to enrol in university and study what she wanted to study, to graduate and work in a respectable profession, and to build a decent future for herself that would compensate her for her past sufferings.

She hesitated to begin the conversation and became preoccupied with caring for Kamela, who was aging and showing signs of disease.

Amal looked back over days past.

Years ago, when Al-Haja arranged for her to work for one of her acquaintances, she could not continue because of unforeseen circumstances. At home and at school, Amal was nervous and troubled because her parents and those around her treated her like a boy. Without her realising, this had an effect on her innermost psychological, nervous, and behavioural formation, as well as the fabric of her relationships with those around her: father, mother, sisters, and the school community in which she was registered as a boy, even though some of those around her, including Al-Haja Kamela, her six sisters, and a few male schoolmates, were aware of the truth about her case and her tragedy.

She became confused at times because of the pressures her parents exerted on her and those around her, and she occasionally fell into a delusion created by those people. When she had epilepsy or schizophrenia-like symptoms, they imposed deterrence, official papers, warnings, and threats on her by force, and she insisted that she was a girl, not a boy. However, she used to notice in such situations that she was screaming and rebelling in a boy's voice and with the emotions of a boy!

When she was alone with herself back then, she would stand in front of a large mirror and ask herself, Is this a boy or a girl?

Every now and then, she was able to shut herself in a room; her parents' bedroom while they were away, staring in the mirror, slowly removing her clothes, piece by piece, revealing herself. She is aware of the physical characteristics of this body. Who said it was a boy?

I'm a girl in every way, sons of bitches. A girl in every way. Criminals come take a look for yourself. Where do you intend to go from here, Goddammit? God will avenge me by punishing you bastards. Why are you torturing me like this? What exactly did I do to you? Is it my sin that you didn't have any sons? You turn me into a boy, you infidels?!

Amal absorbs her pain, extracting what is in her heart and mind, and releasing all anger, pain, sadness, and despair.

She has no idea how many times she fantasized about leaving this world, about escaping her tragedy, her pain, and the torment of every moment and every day. She couldn't count how many times the thought of suicide overwhelmed her. She tried and tried to end this injustice, but she couldn't. There was always a reason why she couldn't commit suicide. Her inability to commit suicide is due to her lack of knowledge of the means and certain things that happened that caused the attempt to be thwarted.

A conflict between her desire as a teenager to embrace life and her hatred for what it was and for those who caused it had resulted in cases of pathological calm and mental and nervous disorientation.

***

A few years went by. Over four years, Amal accomplished what she had not accomplished in all her previous years of life. She completed her university education and studied law through a distance learning system. She now has a strong sense of self-confidence and a deep affection for Al-Haja Kamela, whom she refers to as Mama Kamela. Now, Amal looks at life through a positive lens, anticipating a respectable job worthy of her university diploma. but she also experiences an emotional need that she is unable to express and disclose to Mama Kamela, who is now on the verge of death. Pains, diseases, and memories conspire against her and she is always alone in her large room, which takes up half of the fourth floor. Al-Haja Kamela converses with herself frequently and for long periods of time, as if she were knitting threads on an endless spool.

Amal occasionally succumbs to her tendency to listen in on Al-Haja Kamela's lengthy conversations with herself:

"Woe to you, Sanniya, is this something that parents do to their children? You bury the girl in a boy's mould. You will not be forgiven by God for what you have done. Oh, I warned you not to go with this fool, your husband. There is nothing to be gained.

"Are you saying she's a boy?! On what planet? You wanted a boy, and that jobless father of the girls wanted a boy too. Why? What's wrong with girls? Aren't you one of us? I've always said that you've been disappointed and in a great deal of turmoil, but praise be to God, our Lord has rescued Amal from your and Adawi's oppression. The most important thing I've done in my life is to save her from the grave you dug for her. You'll know what kind of insult you inflicted on her over the years if you see her beauty, her luminous face, and the spirit that has returned to her here.

"Until she enters her married life, I resolved to pay for her education and all her requests, in order to return to her something you denied her with your darkened hearts.

"The problem is that you didn't know how to raise the first six, nor their sister, your youngest, whom you turned into a boy against the will of our Lord, who created her as a girl. I mean, you've been doubly disappointed. Of course, what are you expecting from a frustrated person who has already disappointed you and himself? Al-Usta Sayyid was a true gentleman. Our Lord gave him a house and a wife. She gave birth to sons and daughters for him. I pray that our Lord will soothe your heart, purify it, give you reason and understanding, and forgive your sins, when you repent, move forward, and review yourself and your conscience.

"Lord, please forgive her."

Kamela's journey continued, and she was awake, dreaming of what would happen to her unborn daughter, as she now refers to her, and who would be the man who would suit her and take her to the future she dreamed of.

Amal found herself wanting to express herself in writing for some reason, perhaps because she was missing friends or someone she could trust or be reassured by; she needed someone her own age or generation, and staying with Mama Kamela all the time put her in the position of younger daughter, and she was looking forward to being bigger than that, aspiring to express her femininity, maturity, and openness.

Al-Haja Kamela and Naima, her only daughter, are the only people around. I can't tell her frankly what's inside of me, and I'm not confident in her ability to understand or her honesty in keeping the secret. There's no getting away from the fact that paper, pens, and notebooks keep secrets and open their pages to you without condition or restriction. They do not gatekeep, do not oppose you, stop you talking, discourage you or your thoughts and dreams, offend you, or hurt your feelings. To paper, then.

Amal's first attempts to write her thoughts, ideas, obsessions, fears, and dreams floundered. Her ability to express herself by words was hampered by her feelings and emotions about the turmoil in her heart. She scribbles and then scribbles, again and again.

She decided to find something to read: a book, a novel, a magazine, anything that would serve as a guide and an instructor, from which style, language, words, and formulations could be derived.

She found nothing but an old book written in dense language, eloquent and antique, in Al-Haja Kamela's house. There was no hope in the textbooks that clutter her room. They will not help her express herself. All of them are textbooks, not literary works.

She's looking for a book that would help her become more fluent and allow her hand to relax when she tries to write again. Where would you find such a book?

Amal thinks.

What did Mama Kamela do wrong? She pays for all my living and educational expenses from high school to university level out of her own pocket. I'm not sure if she's my mother or my father. She is more beloved than both of my parents combined. Lord, please help me quickly repay her for some of her kindnesses before death snatches her away from me. She's about to come to an end. Lord, please extend her life so that I can repay her favour. Some of her generosity and grace.

Mama Kamela made sacrifices so that I could attend university and receive a degree. She claims that I am the first child of the family to attend university in its history. She tells me stories and tales about the family's generations, how they drowned in the muck of life, their abandonment of education from the start, and their early entry into the labour market. She curses the poor, destitute, illiterate, stupidity, hopeless, and powerless.

***

Amal benefited greatly from education. She felt compelled to have a better future than her sisters, who had lost all hope of social advancement and had received no formal education. Their mother forced most of them to help her in the houses where she worked as a housemaid, and they later moved on to other houses to work.

Amal's parents agreed that she should attend school for a peculiar reason: their insistence on treating her as a boy, and their fear that the matter would be exposed if she worked at home with her mother, and it turned out that she was a girl, not a boy, as they claimed. Another reason was that they wanted no more girls. The most compelling reason is that the mother's and sisters' labour generated income, allowing the family to pay for Amal's education.

The truth is that the girls were witnessing and attempting to alleviate Amal's suffering, and missing a week or more of school was overcoming a curse, and their first dreams come true. Against her parents' wishes, she moved in with her aunt, Kamela.

Although Adawi, Amal's father, was overjoyed by her departure, he had to pretend to object and not welcome it, even object to her lack of obedience and her fleeing to her aunt Kamela's arms and care. But he also knew that she would be honest to herself and come into her femininity under her aunt's care, so he agreed with Sanniya that she would not try to retrieve her.

As a result, he issued a secret decree to his family, his wife, and daughters, telling them not to try to retrieve Amal.

***

I'd always wished to be free of my suffering.

They've called me Amal since I was a little schoolgirl in my youth. The last of the bunch.

But they were all against me.

My father, mother, and six sisters are treating me as a male. I know I am a girl, not a boy. My mother knows, my father knows, and they all know, but they treat me like a boy, even putting on my birth certificate Amal —Gender: Male!

I am inexperienced and naive. I was a boy, of course, playing with the boys and dressing in boy's clothes, and they first cut my hair to be as short as a boy's hair.

My aunt Kamela was the only one who acknowledged that I was a girl and refused to treat me as a boy. She knew that something had occurred between my mother and father and Sithom, the midwife, whom my aunt despises and sees as the source of all my misery.

After my mother's parents, our grandfather and grandmother, died, my aunt Kamela became the head of her family. She is a real woman with a dead husband. She calls one-eyed people one eyed to their face. She felt sorry for me because of the abuse and cruelty I had received from everyone, including my six sisters, who all knew I was a female with all their feminine features. My father's and mother's brutality drove them all to cede to their desperate desire to have a son after so many daughters.

When my father returned home and learned that the new-born was a girl, he was embarrassed.

My aunt Kamela once told me that after the birth of my third sister, Heba, my father considered getting rid of her. He told my mother, in a fit of rage, addressing her as if she was the one behind the girls, that he didn't want girls. Even this third one, he didn't want her, and that if she left her in front of a mosque, that would be better for her.

My father left the house, she said, and no one knew where he went. She doesn't recall whether this occurred after the birth of Atta, my fourth sister, or Haniyeh, my fifth sister. The important thing is that Mama Kamela informed me that my father Adawi's disappearance had caused a big problem. Sanniya, my mother, was out of work due to pregnancy and childbirth, and we didn't have any other resources at the time besides what she was earning as a domestic worker. Only Mama Kamela could save us from starvation. She was widowed following the death of her husband, and she inherited some money, and this house, which she now lives in and rents out part of. During my father's absence and disappearance, she moved in with us, but I was not among them, as I had not yet been born.

It's as if he didn't exist in both his absence and presence.

My aunt repeats herself. I inquired: "What happened next? How did my father return? What happened to him?"

"Because he was unemployed at the time, this caused an argument. He could not find work. He was angry at your mother, so he joined a group of unemployed and aimless people and lived in their company, and they all do drugs."

"But where did you get all this information?"

"Didn't I tell you, my darling, that I had opened my house to the residents of the lane at the time. All the hanging birds, from whom I learned everything, even the sound of an ant's footfall reached me."

Although the girl has completed her university studies, she is listed as a boy in her university papers—according to her birth certificate, which Kamela had to pay a fee to get a copy of.

Amal had a happy university life as an irregular student who was listed on the affiliation lists but occasionally attended lectures. She was content because no one knew about her problem. Everyone treated her as if she were a young woman, a university student.

She studied law. She isn't sure why she decided to study law, but her subconscious mind was undoubtedly behind it. She was deprived of her rights for a long time in her father's home. Mama Kamela may have offered some encouragement toward it.

She did not experience the same level of distress at university as she did at her parents' home. She is now a university student, a well-known young lady who has attracted the attention and care of several male and female classmates, including her neighbours in the area and even those in Hanging Bird Lane.

Amal is now sitting alone at home, at the home of Mama Kamela, who is also lying in her bed, suffering from multiple diseases besides the normal aches and pains of old age. Naima, her cousin, had returned from some errand that Amal was unaware of on the ground floor. Maybe she went to fetch al-Haja Kamela some medicine that her mother's doctor had prescribed to relieve her pain and calm her mind.

It occurred to her that she should go see Mama. She felt like she had been neglecting Kamela, not reassuring her or fulfilling her requests for a long time.

She required drink, food, and medicines. She didn't move, and Amal noticed that she hadn't moved or said anything for a long time. She looked like a stone, clay, or wax statue!

Sometimes she found her in a complete stupor, her eyes wide open to the maximum extent possible, and her mouth half closed and half open, but she doesn't speak. She speaks without making a sound, and her thick, wrinkled lips do not move.

It's as if she's speaking to someone familiar, whom she sees with her imaginary eyes, but Amal doesn't see him. She addresses God directly as Amal heard her do at the beginning of her last worsening illness. Not only that, Amal recalls Kamela drowning in a state of give-and-take with the Lord of the Worlds.

Then, when she feels normal again, she tells Amal and Naima what happened!

Naima sucks her thick, round lips, which are full of health and vitality, before placing her face between her palms and repeating some prayers and Quranic verses while wiping away the tears that flowed against her will.

Soon after, Kamela solved the mystery that had engulfed Amal and Naima, leaving them befuddled, anxious, and fearful how the changes in her disease or diseases would affect her life. She died peacefully, sleeping in her bed in her favourite room.

Amal and Naima were sitting and talking about simple daily matters, perhaps trivial to fill the time they had spent beside her. When they heard a strong gasp that shook Kamela's weak body and made it shiver. Their entire being and senses were drawn to her.

"Good God!"

Was that the last thing she said? Or did she exclaim something like "goodbye"?

Neither Amal nor Naima could confirm which she said, they were in a state of stupor, loss, sadness, and shock unlike any other. Although they and those around them knew that Kamela was bidding farewell to life.

Amal had never felt such a deep sense of bitter sadness before. She had learned of various people's deaths from relatives, neighbours, acquaintances, and even famous artists and others she had seen on film and television.

She had grieved a little here and there, but it was a different grief this time. Sadness is like the sensation of being dead or dying or about to die. Sadness is like a knife in a deep wound, it's heavy.

SIXTH STAGE

Human beings Always
Need Human beings

After the death of Kamela, Amal became despondent, and her job search dragged on in vain. Despite her university degree, she was ashamed and miserable, living alone and unemployed. She was dependent on Naima, her cousin, who would express kindness to her, console her, and tell her to be patient. But how long would it last? And what is Naima's and her family's sin? She needed to look for work.

She was shopping at a nearby grocery store when she noticed an advertisement in the store next door:

Women required for immediate work.

She walked in with her few purchases and inquired after the shop's owner. She considered leaving when the girl who had greeted her inside the shop walked off, but she remembered that she desperately needed any work, so she did not have to rely on what Naima gave her. But she has no idea what the shop's specialty is. What exactly does it sell? Or does it offer services?

She scanned the shop from corner to corner, her eyes absorbing everything. However, she couldn't find the answer to her question!

Nothing could give you any clue that revealed the shop's activity. The items in this strange shop appeared to her to be clutter, the remains of things, boxes, rolls, and cartons, and nothing gave you anything that reveals what the shop was for. One thing, one impression that Amal got was that what she saw was evidence of a shop, but the shop could have changed hands.

A woman approached and said in a warm and welcoming tone, "In a moment, Hajj Shehata will be here to speak to you about everything."

She was getting ready to ask when she heard a man's voice, a melodious voice, as if he were reciting verses from the Noble Qur'an. He hemmed and hawed before saying:

"God's will is final. God's will is final. What's your name, my daughter?"

"Amal, sir."

"Where are you living?"

"Here, sir."

"Are your parents alive?"

(She paused for a moment before telling a lie, perhaps to gain sympathy from the man.)

"Only my father is alive, and I want to work hard and live off the sweat of my brow so that I am not reliant on others."

"Do you have any idea what kind of work we have?"

"No. What?"

"It's actually a very simple task. We are the ones who came up with the idea for a service office."

"What does that mean?"

"We offer the customers house maids."

"Do you want me to work as a housemaid, sir, despite the fact I have a law degree from a university?"

"No, my daughter, God forbid. You'll be the employee we need in the office. We will benefit from your education in our business."

Amal paused for a moment before reaching a conclusion in herself. "But how much will you pay me, sir?"

"At first, it'll be a small wage, but as the operation progresses and our business grows, you'll be paid double. What do you say?"

"What does the start look like? I mean, how much?"

"Ten pounds per day, so 300 pounds per month."

"In a job like this, I won't accept less than a thousand pounds per month. I will be extremely beneficial to the office."

It is astonishing that Hajj did not refuse Amal's request, nor bargain with her. She found herself suddenly employed and earning a handsome amount.

It wasn't long before Amal discovered herself and became the centre of the office activist.

All she has to do is make lists of customers' names, professions, addresses, and phone numbers, as well as the requests they make. She then makes other lists in a different book, including the names of female job applicants, their ages, previous experience, and so on. Married – divorced – widowed – and if she is a mother, how many sons and daughters does she have, and what are their ages? And so forth.

More than one notebook was filled with data, information, names, and addresses after a short period of time. Hajj Shehata discovered that Amal was a gift from heaven after a very short time. She was bright and knew what she was doing from the moment she walked into the office, which he had named *Integrity Office of Sustainable Services* inscribed on a temporary sign.

There are three telephone numbers beneath the name in large font, two of which are answered by Amal and her colleague Hind, and the third is al-Hajj's personal mobile number.

It was natural that Amal knew little about the job at first, and al-Hajj oversaw her education and training.

Al-Hajj transferred all the routine work, answering phones, and using computers, to Samiha, an employee with prior experience in office work, when she arrived, and assigned Amal the basic tasks of coordination, collection, follow-up, and data entry.

It was early in the morning on a sunny day, and the sky was clear when Amal asked him about how he had developed an interest in this type of work. Al-Hajj sat back and began to stroke his prominent belly while reminiscing.

"Oh, praise be to God! What made you think of this question? Allow me to take you back in time. You wouldn't believe me if I told you that my first and only job was through an office like ours.

"And wouldn't you say that I treat you like my daughter and more, and I wouldn't tell you what I'm about to tell you if it weren't for the respect I have for you. You agree, Amal?"

Amal nodded, preparing to listen with longing and anticipation for everything that Hajj would tell her.

Before he opened the course of an unfinished conversation, the man gave her one last look, and his piercing eyes made her feel safe. Driven by a deep desire to tell and recount the story of his life, he set out without stopping, except to suck a mouthful of water from the jug in front of him, or to swallow his saliva, or to dry the sweat running down his forehead.

The gist of what he said was that he was an orphan who had fled from problems in the countryside and that he knew no one in Cairo, and that his first source of income was at a service office, where he worked in the owner's mansion, who was so wealthy that you wondered what the secret of his owning a service office was!

★★★

Days went by. Amal listened to more details of Hajj's life. He told her that the owner of the mansion chose him over others for reasons he didn't understand at the time, and his employer didn't tell him about. He treated him well and only gave him simple tasks that did not merit the monthly wage he paid him.

Pasha's wife, the madam, expressed such concern and sympathy for him that he began to suspect that there was something going on.

What's the point of it all?

Despite his apprehensions, doubts, and mistrust from time to time, he was content. What exactly is the problem? Is there something they're planning for me I don't want? Is there a price I'll have to pay for this kind and suspicious treatment?

He spent days and nights being tossed by winds of apprehension and drowning in whirlpools of anxiety, but feelings of happiness and contentment were like lifeboats that carried him suddenly to safety, only to return again, drown in a sea of mystery.

Then one day he found himself in bed with the madam!

Without warning, Hajj's speech was cut short. The man remained silent, tears welling up in his eyes, and Amal found herself alone in the office for a time. When al-Hajj returned from an adjacent room, Amal was talking to a customer who inquired about the possibility of providing a maid capable of caring for a woman on the verge of death.

Al-Hajj helped go through the office's database to fulfil the customer's request. He also stopped talking about what had happened to him in the madam's bed.

However, Amal used her imagination to complete the story, assuming that the presence of Al-Hajj in the madam's bed did not imply that he was sleeping in bed with her. He couldn't have been old enough to play her secret lover.

But what exactly was he doing in bed at the time?

He might have gone to her with medicine or something because she was sick.

Perhaps the Pasha delivered a message to the madam and sent him while she was resting in bed.

Amal paused for a while. She then went back to her fantasies outside of the bed. She imagined Pasha was on the lookout for a son because he didn't have one. He was afraid that if he died without leaving his property to someone, he could trust his wife would ask him to adopt a son.

Is this how it went down?

No, if all that Amal imagined had happened, al-Hajj would not have needed to open this service office.

Thinking about what might have happened, she said to herself, perhaps Pasha and his wife sympathized with Al-Hajj because they too yearned for a son and wanted to satiate their passion for parenting which went unfulfilled due to their inability to have children. Is it as simple as that?

No, probably not. It's not possible. Is it possible that the man was homosexual? No, because al-Hajj was also treated well by Pasha's wife. Was she also looking for a young man to have a secret relationship with?

When he returned to finish what had been cut off and they were alone in the office, Al-Hajj interrupted her chain of thoughts and fantasies and asked her:

"Are you looking forward to hearing the rest of my story?"

He didn't have to wait for her response because he could read it on her face.

Al-Hajj revealed to her that the man was sympathetic to him, cared about him, and chose him over other workers because he was confident in and reassured by his behaviour, morals, and conduct, which is the secret behind his establishment of this office. He doesn't need any money beyond what he already has in terms of land and real estate. Having a large income, of course, the man and his wife's weakness, childlessness, played a role in the situation, and they used to lavish him with tenderness and kindness.

As he previously explained to Amal, his presence in Madam's bed was due to Pasha sending him to her while she was ill, carrying various types of medicines brought to him by a friend from abroad.

Al-Hajj concluded his speech with an unbelievable story, but he vouched that it occurred as if it were a miracle or a gift from heaven to a young, orphaned man who had been brutally deprived of the chance at a normal life under his parents. With his health deteriorating after the death of his wife, the man summoned al-Hajj and informed him that he had officially registered the will in his name.

He did so in accordance with an agreement he and his wife had reached shortly before she departed.

Amal was sceptical of the strange story. She said it had to be one of this orphan's imaginative creations, and he wanted to have an amazing story to tell about his success. But, when she thought about it later, she checked herself and said that, despite all the troubles and torments she had witnessed so far, the world might be fine.

What al-Hajj told me must be true, since there's no reason for him to lie or fabricate stories that never happened, so whatever he told me had to be true. Why would he exaggerate or lie about things?

Her thoughts, on the other hand, came and went without ever resolving into a situation or reaching a conclusion.

Amal realized she had no family, friends, or acquaintances to whom she could return, open her heart to, seek help from, or discuss her problems and circumstances, hoping to find a solution.

There's only al-Hajj, but is he the right person to talk to about his incredible story?

No, what do you expect from him, Amal? She asked herself, laughing at her own naivety.

She asked him in her exorbitant naiveté.

"Is it true, Hajj, what you're telling me? I'm not sure I believe it! Are there still people in the world like this Pasha you said left everything to you?!"

The man, who was sitting in his opulent shop office, couldn't stop laughing. He takes a breath, then returns with a louder, more wide-ranging, and resonant guffaw.

"You bought into the story?"

"So, you're taking advantage of my naivety and the kindness in my heart by telling me fairy tales that not even children would believe".

The man continued to laugh, and she looked as if she had no idea what was going on, until the laughter stopped, and welling of light tears wet his eyes, prompting him to exclaim:

"Would I lie to you, my daughter? Have you, God forbid, known me to be a liar?"

"God forbid it, sir, but the venerable honour of Pasha leaves someone like me dumbfounded by the truth. Please excuse me, Hajj, I'm sorry. I used to believe that life was harsh, and that people were like that, but I didn't think that you favoured me with a job, promotions, and salary, and I forgot that God gave me you and my friend who saved me from a terrible idea that controlled my being and my aunt Kamela who embraced me and illuminated the way for me, providing me with housing and peace."

It was natural for her to tell him her story, and he listened with his heart in his ears.

Al-Hajj is a sensitive, merciful, kind, and patient man. He developed these characteristics during his tough childhood and youth as an orphan, because he lived in a shelter and had no family, no uncles, or aunts, no grandfather or grandmother, he had to realize in his state of loss that there was no way to survive in this life except through obedience, hard work, and love. He was paying attention intently. He becomes agitated in some situations, then calms down and continues to listen.

Amal noticed that she was telling her story differently this time from the way she had told Inshirah. She doesn't exaggerate or make up events, and she doesn't fabricate things that didn't happen to her. Is it because she considers Hajj to be a straightforward, honest, and kind man toward whom she has no negative feelings? He does not frighten her. She does not feel that he has any dubious intentions toward her; they are all distinct feelings from the ones she experienced and overcame as she told Inshirah!

Is it because Inshirah was mysterious, strong-willed, and self-reliant for a long time, and because of her toughness and plasticity in the face of life's challenges?!

Al-Hajj did not choose to be orphaned; it was fate's will. Inshirah is the one who chose to be an orphan by fleeing her family and severing ties with them after they had harmed her and imprisoned her.

But, after that, what happened to Hajj Shehata? What was the outcome of his life's journey? Do you know if he's married or not? Is he the father of any children? So far, none of this has been mentioned in his stories. I need to find out from him. He has a special place in my heart.

Getting close to him, asking for his help, and trusting in his wisdom and kindness of heart may have helped me solve some of my problems.

I believe he is my real father, the father I deserved, my long-lost father, and the one who had gone missing.

Al-Hajj surprised me by inquiring about my plans for the future.

Does he believe I'm capable of answering such a question?

"The truth is, sir, I have no idea!"

The good man was taken aback and burst into laughter.

"You are strange, my daughter. Someone your age, you have the entire world in front of you, and you have no idea what you want in the future."

The good man's words and his resonant laugh from deep within his heart moved me to tears, and after a long moment of silence, I found myself speaking.

He listened eagerly and pityingly, contemplating my face, the movement of my hands, and all my gestures, smiling and repeating prayers, vows, or words, I'm not sure what, as he mumbled as if praying.

Office requirements cut my story short, so he decided, without even asking me about my conditions after hours, to invite me to lunch in a nearby restaurant in the Sayeda area, to continue the story, and so he could continue to listen.

He was speaking as if he had found a case he wanted to elucidate, and I had nothing to stop me from indulging him, not only because I love trotters, head meat, mumbar, and behariz soup, but also because I love this man's tenderness.

We went to a famous hotel after lunch, and al-Hajj told me that it was the best place for him to listen to the details of my story with no one disturbing our session.

I felt anxious; does he intend to take advantage of his position as an employer paying me a high salary to entice me? Is his claiming to care about me and my story, him being a wolf in sheep's clothing?

However, the hotel is a public space, and none of this can occur there. I will request and insist that we sit in the lobby so that we can be among people.

But will I be able to do so, or will al-Hajj's sense of influence and superiority over me strengthen his sense of dominance over me, allowing him to control me and force me to submit to him?

I will let no one make me a victim of their sick desires. I will not allow any being to harm me, overstep themselves with me, or exploit my need for stability and reliance on myself, in violation of my being.

He pushed me into a secluded corner of the large hall.

As we sat in these comfortable seats, he summoned one of the hostesses and asked me what I wanted in front of her, with respect and affection, and after a few words, he repeated them to reassure me Then he told me of the place he said he used to run away to sit alone by himself.

I spoke on and on and on, and Hajj Shehata listened intently, encouraging me to tell him more boring details. As I continued to speak, I had the impression that I was being opening myself. I reflect on everything that has occurred. I also have a sense of strength.

The strange thing is that the man didn't interrupt me, didn't ask for details, and constantly surrounded me with feelings I'd never experienced from another human being. Even Mama Kamela surrounded me with different emotions, though I couldn't explain why.

When I finished my long story, which was only interrupted by a second request for drinks and juice, al-Hajj sighed and said in an angel's voice, "This is how I received it: with much paternity and magnanimity.

"My daughter, the world is still fine, and our Lord's provision is plentiful, and all I want to tell you is that our Lord has given me a lot, but you are the most precious gift from God to me.

"What has happened to you has been difficult and has involved cruelty, brutality, and injustice, but what is to come is all good, happiness, and insouciance. Perhaps God sent you to me for you to help me and me to help you. Human beings always need Human beings."

SEVENTH STAGE

Reclaiming my Lost Femininity

Amal was once again bereaved. Fate had surprised her yet again. She could no longer work in the office after Hajj Shehata died, and what the man left to her transformed her into a business owner, i.e. a businesswoman, not just a service office manager, but also a property owner.

Al-Hajj had prepared well for the day he would leave this world and, as happened to him many years ago, when he was surprised that his employer had transferred ownership of everything to him, he left everything he owned to Amal.

It took her a long time to organize her situation, but she didn't realize just how long.

For her, the most important thing was to live her life. She had lost an age in getting rid of her parents and restoring her original being as a female, so circumstances in recent years had not allowed her to get to know a person she could love and eventually marry. Only those who were looking for a house maid came to the office. Either elderly people who required someone to care for them, or young husbands in search of someone to look after their children during the parents' working hours. Those were not suitable for marriage or even love!

She cannot marry through a matchmaker because she is looking for a man, not a commodity that you need an intermediary to obtain.

With her ownership of the office and the property left to her by Hajj Shehata, she has become a businesswoman, making the situation more difficult. Everyone who proposes to her, or most of them, will be under suspicion. Is he interested in marrying Amal for herself or for what she possesses?

She thought of the maze into which she had fallen and had to spend months trying to find her way out of this vortex.

What do you do? Do you give in to the idea of hiring a matchmaker? Or does she look for her own groom? Do you use newspapers or the Internet to advertise suitable groom needed! Could she be considering going through her friends?

Should she, in this case, abandon the idea of marriage entirely?

She has been looking for a long time and has found nothing. All that surrounds her is confusion. To avoid it, she deliberately ignores the entire situation, lives moment by moment, and becomes preoccupied with other issues that do not raise questions or cause confusion. She can now handle that.

In an instant, an idea arose in her head and took control of her entire being. She was walking down a downtown street, passing in front of a tourism and aviation office, on her way to a store where she planned to buy a dress in a window that had caught her eye the last time she walked down the same street.

She came to a halt in front of a billboard visible through the airline's window. A large image of Big Ben, the famous London clock and tower.

Amal believed that the solution to all her problems lay in this location. London.

It's a foreign country, and I'll be an outsider there. Nobody knows Amal, and Amal knows no one.

New beginnings, starting with a new life.

However, there is an obstacle on the way to London.

Amal, said to herself, you are conversant with the English language. But not nearly enough to live with the English people.

A simple problem to solve. I only require three months. An intensive language course, then my journey to a new journey begins, and a new life will be written for me.

What should I do now?

Sell everything and get ready for my new life. I'll spend my new life learning everything I can about this country, its people, and everything else. I'll go to the British Council and ask all my questions before enrolling in a language course.

I have a few months before my life begins, which I am now planning on my own.

***

London wasn't anything like what I'd learned!

What the British Council, where I studied speaking, reading, and writing in the language impeccably, taught me about the capital, which I arrived at yesterday, was different from what I had seen. When I arrived in the middle of the day, all I saw was darkness, as if we were at night. Despite the cold weather, there was hustle and bustle in the streets. If I were in Egypt with this weather, I wouldn't see anyone out on the streets.

Did I fall prey to the tourist propaganda given to me about London while studying at the British Embassy-affiliated centre?

They said it was a clean city, which pleased me because cleanliness is a sign of civilization, but I was surprised when I arrived in the heart of the big city and smelt foul odours everywhere, and when the taxi took me from the airport, I discovered row upon row in almost all the streets along the sidewalks, and sometimes piles of huge black plastic bags. I did not know what their secret was, and I was too embarrassed to ask the taxi driver. I didn't want him to know I was visiting for the first time. I was concerned that if he found that information, it would put me in jeopardy.

My mind remained troubled.

I discovered the reason by accident the next day. I tried to purchase something from a small shop on the corner of a cinema near the hotel where they had reserved a room for me. What should I purchase? The hotel provides food, and I don't smoke, drink alcohol, or like chocolate. I decided to buy some fruits after seeing them as I entered the shop. Apples, bananas, grapes, and even watermelon!

This shop is odd. It is not a supermarket or a tuck shop, but it sells bottles of wine and cigarettes, as well as sandwiches with vegetables and fruit!

Unpleasant odours haunt me. Is this how London welcomes me?

Though I said nothing, the old salesperson, noticing my disgust at the horrible smells, told me in a heavy and difficult English accent:

"Please accept my apologies. Cleaners in London have been on strike for several days. They allowed us to smell this "fresh air", a taste of French joy for us." He fell silent after laughing in a way that made me feel stupid, then returned to me and said, "Don't worry, dear, they will force the government to respond to their demands after a day or two. We forgive them really. They can't very well clean the city while their pockets are empty!"

He said it ironically, and I understand it with difficulty. The man speaks English fluently and with a distinct accent that is difficult for me to work out.

Although he was engaged in conversation with another man when I entered the shop, he was completely free to entertain me for the short period I spent in his clean and elegant shop. I noticed that he was staring at me with eyes narrowed in amazement!

When I went to pay for my items, he asked me affectionately about my country of origin, possibly because of my brown skin and possibly because I was disgusted by the smell, although it had apparently been there for a while, and, of course, because of my English pronunciation. When he found out I was Egyptian, he was delighted and spoke with a warmth that the English people are not known for, and he told me he had an Egyptian aunt!

Of course, I wasn't convinced.

The old Englishman's keen eye noticed that there were signs of doubt on my face about what he was saying, so he exclaimed, "You do not believe me, but it's true. She is, of course, English, because she is my late father's sister; his little sister, a nurse who married an Egyptian doctor who was studying here, and when he finished his studies, he took her to Egypt with him. Of course, that was over a quarter-century ago, before you were born.

He was laughing hysterically, which I thought was unwarranted.

Old Harry is a nice guy, and his false teeth almost fall out of his mouth when he laughs. He laughs as if it were his last chance to laugh. He knew a lot about me while I knew almost nothing about him. He was happy to assist me with anything because I was from his aunt's country!

He surprised me by leaving the shop and returning with a cup of tea and a sandwich cut into small triangles on a plate. and an antique picture in a frame, and exclaimed within earshot of his friend, who did not speak very much, saying:

"This is my Egyptian aunt Georgette, and on behalf of my wife Harriet, this is our hospitality and celebration of you. She is inside and she'd love to meet you. Come on, through here."

I was confused because I am unfamiliar with this country and its people, and I am unaware of their rituals, inclinations, and intentions, and I did not know what would happen to me here. However, I left my purchased items and entered the room.

The woman, who greeted me as if she'd known me for years, was young for her husband, Harry. I wouldn't say she's nearly the same age as his daughter; she's a little older, but she's still young!

I had barely sat down on the seat she indicated when old Harry appeared behind me, carrying the tea and the plate of small triangular sandwiches that I had left outside.

Harriet had taken a seat across from me, her tea, and sandwiches beside her.

She laughed and said, "Harry prefers beer or coffee to tea. That's why he sometimes abandons me in favour of his favourite beer. Tell me about yourself, my dear. To begin, what's your name? He never mentioned it to me."

"Amal," I said.

"Does it mean something?" she inquired.

I explained the meaning in English to her, and she expressed her admiration for my name. She expressed hope that one day she could visit Egypt with Harry. "Your country is incredible, Amal," she elongated the pronunciation of my name so that became Amal.

"I hope that happens as soon as possible," I said. "Egypt is magnificent."

Harriet told me about various things over tea and sandwiches, including the fact that she lived upstairs, above the shop, and that she used to work in that shop before she married Harry, after his first wife died in an accident.

"He's a good and generous man who makes me laugh, which is all I want in a man."

For a moment, there was silence. Perhaps she was putting together memories of her life, and I was telling myself that good fortune had brought me together with good people, perhaps to ease the feelings of homesickness that had swept over me from the moment the plane touched down at Heathrow Airport.

But Harriet soon spoke again, asking if I am on a trip as a tourist or for study.

I told her that I actually intended to stay here.

"Did you get the necessary permit?" she asked.

I explained that I came here with the help of the embassy and the British Council on a one-year scholarship that can be extended based on the study programme.

"What kind of studies?"

"English Literature and language. I am permitted to include additional materials after consulting with the grant supervisor here."

"But just because you're studying here, doesn't mean you get residency."

"I know, and I intend to apply for permanent residency later."

"Welcome to your second home, Amal."

I gave them my phone number and the address of the hotel, and they gave me a card with the name of the shop and Harry's name and phone number, and I thanked them and expressed my gratitude for introducing themselves to me, and I promised to come back. They said goodbye to me as I left the shop. Even their silent friend said my name when he said goodbye to me.

***

The hotel is like a youth hostel, and this type is known as Bed and Breakfast here.

I discovered a way to use the hotel's computer for an hourly fee. I wanted to use this magical device to pass the time in this boring freezing weather. The cold here is more than just the cold weather, but I'm not feeling it right now because I'm in my warm room. All the hotel's rooms and public areas are warm, and central heating is ubiquitous. I noticed it in Harry's store and even in the taxi.

Despite the devices spreading warmth and expelling coldness, I feel the coolness of the treatment here in this small hotel. Almost no one speaks to the guests. Although the vast majority of them appear to be English rather than foreigners or strangers such as myself.

I worked with the computer, and after several failed attempts and errors with search engines, I was able to gain control over the situation and get a wealth of useful information.

Because the hotel, Simplicity—a funny and comfortable name—only serves breakfast, I had to go out to find dinner, and for lunch, I was provided with small triangular sandwiches coincidentally like the ones Harry had brought for me and were prepared by his young wife, Harriet.

The hotel employee advised me not to eat at any of the nearby restaurants because they are all "touristy". He suggested that I should go shopping and prepare dinner in the hotel kitchen.

He believes that I am a student with only enough money for myself. He does not know that I am wealthy, and that I have enough money to last me for years without having to work.

Of course, I will tell no one here. Who knows what would happen if someone discovered my secret?

I kept playing on the computer, and I was amused and entertained, but what is the news in Egypt?

This device is only available in English. I considered purchasing my own computer and requesting that the Arabic language program be installed alongside the English language.

Now, I'll take the hotel employee's advice. I'm not sure what his name was. I was on my way to the supermarket I had been told to get what I needed for dinner. But then I thought, why not stop by Harry and Harriet first and see if I can find my things with them or have them solve this dinner problem?

Perhaps I'll be overcome by laziness, so I can cut it short and buy a sandwich from their shop.

Harry wasn't there. Harriet told me he had gone shopping, and I noticed this quiet young man, whose name I don't know.

Harriet invited me to sit with her in her room. I left the young man dealing with the customers alone. I'm not sure why I had a hunch that this silent one had some connection to Harriet, but I didn't try to bring it up to her.

A while passed without my asking what I could make myself for dinner. Harriet would occasionally leave me to look around the shop and speak briefly with the silent person before returning to join my company. I told myself that he was probably her brother or a relative, because their audible conversation had a familiarity and smoothness you rarely hear between an employer and an employee.

Harry arrived and escorted the silent man to his car to retrieve the goods. I stayed in the shop with Harriet. She interacts with customers, accepts their money, issues receipts, and gives them their change. And she put their purchases in bags. Although most customers are strangers who are probably coming into the store for the first time, like me, there are regular customers. They are known to Harry, his wife, and the silent young man. What is his name?

I don't want to ask because I might appear to be overly interested in him.

While Harriet is inside, I speak with Harry, who has unloaded the goods and he silently was stacking them in place and sticking on small price tags.

When the young wife comes back, whispering to her husband that dinner is ready, she turns to me and asks, "Would you like to taste my cooking? Come on, you deserve a new English meal. I'd love to hear what you think, Amal."

I laughed at how she pronounced my name and I was astounded by this family, who had only known me for a few hours and had served me lunch and now dinner?

Am I a member of their family? No, but didn't Harry tell me about his Egyptian aunt? Maybe they think of me as family?!

When Harry and I went in for dinner, the young man was left alone in the shop.

Harriet gave me this strange dish. Of course, I had never tried it. I had never even heard of it before!

As she handed it to me, she said, "You'll love this English dish. We call it 'jacket potato', it's delicious, easy, and healthy. Try it and tell me."

In the dish in front of me is a large baked potato, slit lengthwise and crosswise, topped with butter and grated Romano cheese, topped with a portion of minced meat cooked with red kidney beans.

I said to myself in Arabic, "something that opens the soul" and then translated it for them. Harriet's face lit up. "Enjoy my favourite dish, then."

It was really a delicious dish. What my host and her husband told me about their country, their lives, and the young man who is now sitting in the shop was the most delicious of all. The stories are lengthy and entertaining, and I learned from them that they had known each other for many years and that she had met the late wife by chance, and she had asked her to work in the shop. Because Harriet was a stranger from the countryside, Harry and his wife welcomed her and gave her a room in their apartment above the shop.

As for this silent young man, whose name I now know is Tony, he had been a customer of the shop and worked in an office next door, and it just so happened that Harry was looking for someone to help him after the unexpected death of his first wife when Tony lost his job, and despite knowing nothing except office work, he expressed his agreement to work there and Harry also agreed to hire him.

I learned all of this, but I couldn't figure out why he was always silent. The couple said nothing to me, and I found myself unable to ask the question.

Even though I was enjoying their company, anecdotes, and sound advice, I had to return to the hotel.

***

The picture of my life that I'm looking at in my room by myself engrossed me. The most important fact about me is that I am female. Everyone treats me as a woman. A young Egyptian woman. I promised myself that I would prioritize my femininity. Would I be able to deal with the cold, dreary weather of this country that doesn't see the sun?!

So, what will happen to me in class? Will I accomplish anything worthwhile in it? Do I actually want to study English literature? Was it just the country of the literature that I desired?

What should I do after I've finished my studies? What kind of work am I going to do? Which occupation?

Most importantly, will I fall in love here? Will I get married? Egyptian or English?

My many questions bothered me, and my head hurt, so I decided to set them aside for the meantime and get on with moving forward and living. I'll be going to the university in a few days to enrol and inquire about my study programme from the professor in charge of supervising me, and all I have to do now is prepare for that, and above all, I need to learn the lay of this city where I've come to live. I restarted the computer and began looking for something to assist me in my exploration of London.

I was exhausted. I laid down on the bed and felt at ease. Should I go to sleep? I was aware of my body. I wanted to see it naked.

I decided to take a shower, prepared myself and my belongings, and proceeded to the shared bathroom.

The only thing that I was concerned about at the time was to feel my femininity, letting go of the past, and forgetting the agony I had endured. Not sure if I was a boy or a girl. I'm by myself. I take off my clothes and feel the contours of my body, and an unprecedented sense that I really was female washes over me. I really started feeling this way while under Mama Kamela's care. But now I feel something else. In Egypt, I was afraid that someone would harm me because I was registered on the national ID card as a male, although I worked and ran businesses and owned real estate and had the money left to me by Hajj Shehata, and this man, the angel, understood my circumstances and treated me as his daughter, and when he wrote his will, he left his property to me before his death, without my knowledge, but he did not forget that I was registered as male in official papers. This is an exceptional human being who soothed my heart with his generous treatment and assured me by his behaviour toward me and all his actions that the world was fine.

Why are my feelings different now? Why do I find myself in a better condition? Is it because I began a new life away from the sources of my suffering? Who knew London would turn out to be the paradise I'd been looking for my entire life?

In the bathroom, I lingered, enjoying the warmth, the freshness, the sense of self. I now feel like a beautiful, strong, educated young woman with better days and years ahead of her, but will I be happy here although I have no family, acquaintances, friends, or girlfriends? Why wasn't it decreed that I be allowed to live a normal life in my country with my family, sisters, and other relatives?

What happened to my sisters? How are they? This is a curse that has been written on me and will not be removed, the curse of separation and parting from loved ones.

Despite the whirlpool of questions that surrounded me, I remained in the bathroom for a long time, relaxed and enjoying myself.

While drying myself, I looked in the small mirror in front of the sink at my face and chest. I wanted to contemplate my entire body, so I decided to stay naked and wrap myself in the robe I had entered the bathroom in, before returning to my room where the large mirror in the cupboard awaited me to enjoy, undress, and rejoice in my new being.

I moved quickly, carrying my belongings between the bathroom and my room, and the thought of looking at myself in the mirror gripped my mind. When I stumbled on the hem of the robe, someone appeared in the narrow corridor, most likely one of the guests. As the robe slipped off my body and fell to the ground with me, he came towards me to assist. In my haste to leave the bathroom, I didn't bother putting on the robe; I just wrapped myself in it, and my foot caught on its hem, causing the robe to slip. Suddenly, I was stood naked, and this man rushed towards me. I quickly wrapped the robe around myself, but I was still half-naked, almost naked.

I was humiliated and ashamed, and I had no idea what to do. The man approached me and assisted me in standing while allowing me to cover my body. He expressed his relief that I was not hurt and introduced himself:

"Peter Cook. I live here in room 12, and I believe you live in room 14, right?"

"Thank you for your help," I stammered. "I'm sorry. My name is Amal Samahi, and I live in room 14."

He laughed while talking aloud to himself. "I was right. You live in room 14."

I had stood up and was about to continue walking towards my room when I got a strange feeling after a man had seen me naked or semi-naked, and I hurried away.

I caught my breath in the room and my desire to see my naked body, which I assumed Peter had enjoyed sneaking a look at, was heightened. A man had seen my naked body for the first time in my life. Despite my confusion, I nevertheless noticed his admiration for what he saw!

Some moments passed during which I was preoccupied with this incident for a while, contemplating my body, my beauty in front of me in the long mirror on the inside of the cupboard door.

Light knocks on the room's door, interrupting my thoughts and narcissism, and my self-pleasure.

I wrapped myself in the robe once more but decided not to open the door. Who could be knocking? What do they want? I don't know anyone here.

The knocks, however, continued, accompanied by a voice asking: "Amal. Are you alright?"

I pushed open the door. It was the man who saw me naked and came to my aid.

He offered me a drink, claiming that it would help relieve my shock and that it would help me. I took a drink and thanked him from behind the closed door.

He stated that he was in his room if I needed anything. He offered to buy me whatever drink I would like in the bar next door if I wanted. All I had to do was knock on Room 12's door.

I thanked him and replied, "I'm not sure. I'll see."

I'm not sure why I was overcome with a sense of strength or perhaps confidence. What would happen if I sat with a man when the only thing I know about him are his name, that he is my hotel neighbour, that he is generous and gentle, and of course that he saw me naked?!

I need to communicate with others, so the argument within myself took a long time before I responded.

I quickly changed into appropriate clothing, checked how I look, and applied perfume before knocking on the door of number 12.

However, he wasn't ready to go out; he'd stripped down to his underwear and was half naked! He doubted I would accept his invitation, and actually, he didn't open the shutter door when he realized it was me, instead he popped his head from behind the door and said, "one minute and I will be with you".

We had a good time in a nearby pub. It was my first visit to a pub, which is both a café and a restaurant. He ordered his favourite beverage, a sticky, fermented black beer, and after I apologized for not drinking, he agreed to my request for a fresh orange juice.

Peter appeared to be a good and strange being, but it was his profession that made me suspicious. He did something I didn't even know existed. He was a model scout. When he told me about his work, he added a sentence to it that he said automatically: "But I'm not working right now. Don't worry, I won't ask you to join our agency."

I kept questioning him about his work, not because I was interested, but so that I wouldn't be in the crosshairs of his questions, and in this way, I avoided revealing my secrets, so that he knew little about me.

Of course, he had no idea about my suffering before I arrived in London, nor did he know about my small fortune. He didn't know that there was a tick in the 'male' box on my passport. But Peter is overly kind, polite, and gentle. I noticed he didn't flirt with me or make any comments about my naked body. He made no hint, not even a smidgeon, of me joining the agency where he works, which specializes in providing models for fashion houses and advertising agencies, and I learned a lot from him about this exciting profession.

But I was surprised, and an important question occupied my mind: "How is it you say you're looking for beautiful women to be hired in fashion shows and other events, and you help choose filming locations, yet you live in a hotel that's literally called Simplicity?"

He was not surprised by the question. He simply stated that he does not live in the hotel, that he arrived a few days ago, and that he will only stay for a few days.

In fact, I couldn't feel that it is a convincing answer. But I didn't want to embarrass him. So, why am I so interested in this Peter?

Is it because he's the first man to see my naked body? Is it because I desperately need to experience my femininity through a man? Is it because he is generous, kind, and polite? Or because he works in a field that is directly linked to femininity and beauty. Fame, lights, and a lot of money?!

After a few days, Peter invited me to accompany him on one of his work assignments, a trip to Richmond Park, which he described as one of the largest royal parks open to the public, with an area the size of a London neighbourhood and herds of deer living in it. It also has a ballet institute and a botanical research centre and playgrounds for children. I welcomed the invitation, and we spent a day from dawn to dusk in an amazing garden and I watched and experienced the world of models and their work. The assignment was to photograph them with deer, in the garden, during games, and having fun with the kids. They wore clothes designed by one of the international fashion houses in all the shots. I learned that these images, which were captured on video and with photographic cameras, were to be part of a new advertising campaign that would be launched in various media outlets around the world, including television, magazines, and newspapers.

It was a unique method for Peter to show me the world he wanted to draw me into. This experience made me happy, but would I want to be one of these lovely ladies?

I'm not sure. I'm confused. Not just right now, I've always been confused. I'm not sure what I want right now. This is London, which seduced me like a siren from the moment I passed by the tour company's window in Cairo and saw the Big Ben clock tower, so first and foremost, I'd like to see Big Ben.

I was sitting alone and completely naked. I'm rolling around on my bed in my room. I told myself, I must visit Big Ben, which is what brought you here.

★★★

In the morning, the room phone rang. I was astounded!

Who knows what my room number is? Nobody except Peter, but why would he use the phone if he is my neighbour in the room next to mine?!

I picked up the phone without saying hello and heard a familiar voice. It was Harriet asking how I am and why I've been away from her and the shop, and saying that Harry is concerned about you as well.

The only thing I said was: "I am on my way".

I figured Harry and Harriet needed a break from their usual types of entertainment, so they thought why not bring this Egyptian girl and hang out with her? That way, we'd all have something new and exciting to look forward to. I assumed they agreed on this idea right away, and I could be wrong: they might need me for something else I don't know about!

They weren't alone; Tony was there as well. When Harriet and I entered the inner room, she whispered to me—I'm not sure why she was whispering in my ear—we were the only two people in the room.

"Have you ever considered leaving the B&B—I mean, the hotel—and moving in with us in the room I used to live in before Harry's ex-wife passed away! Do you like the idea? It won't cost you much, possibly less than a B&B, and you'd have some additional benefits. The food is full board—that is, three full meals— and there are no annoying guests, aside from our company, of course, and most importantly, my dear Amal, that you will live in the English manner you say you love." Of course, she said it all in fitful sentences, relentless and whispered!

"Why are you whispering?!"

"So that Tony can't hear us."

"So, what if he hears us?"

She laughed softly, almost silently, while saying, "He'll be envious. He's been trying to get the room for years, and Harry has objected to having another man in the house besides him for years."

She paused to catch her breath and then said, "What are your thoughts, my dear?"

"I'm not sure. First and foremost, thank you for thinking of me. Second, I need some time to think and arrange my affairs, and I won't start to do that until I go to the university and I find out what my schedule, appointments, and obligations are, and then I will arrange myself. It is a wonderful idea and generous of you both, so I am grateful, but it is an unexpected idea that did not occur to me. Give me some time, Harriet, and I'll give you my answer."

I wasn't whispering, and she was pointing at me with her finger over her mouth, indicating that I should lower my voice slightly.

She still wore the same smile with which she had greeted me first time, but I wondered, Will Tony not know later when I agree and come to stay here?

We were having tea and cake when Harry arrived, went to the fridge, opened a can of beer for himself, sat down, and said to me, "Did you like the idea?"

Harriet spoke first, and explained to him that, while I liked the idea, I needed some time to think about it, and she didn't forget to tell him that I appreciated their interest.

Harry wasn't whispering at all!

Even Harriet stopped whispering when she spoke first and explained it to him before leaving us to help Tony and the clients.

Harry surprised me by whispering: "I'm hoping you'll agree so we can stop Tony's constant asking for the room."

I whispered: "I'll try to think about it quickly."

Our conversation turned to my situation, and I told him that in a few days I would be attending university and beginning my studies, as well as arranging housing. Then I told him what came to mind spontaneously:

"But first, I need to get to know this exciting city."

He laughed and replied, "You reminded me of something Harriet said to my late wife and me when we hired her to help in the shop. She was from the countryside and had little knowledge of London."

He continued to laugh quietly, saying, "Do you think she explored London and its landmarks after all these years? She was completely immersed in my work. Our work here requires all the hours God sends.

It prevents us from sleeping, save for a few hours."

***

"Amal, life is all confusion."

She said to herself, completely naked and alone on the bed, the mirror of the cupboard facing her, concerned about the unknown future. Her thoughts about herself were wrapped in confusion. Is she confirming her femininity or not? Do you stay in Simplicity or move to live with Harry and Harriet? Is there something more to their offer? Do you attend university and begin a new life, or what?

Is she more interested in the generous Peter or the silent Tony?!

The crashing waves of confusion drag her into a whirlpool, erasing her general sense of happiness and pride in her femininity. Was it a mistake for me to come here? What awaits me in this strange land?

She returned her gaze to the folds of her body. What is all this beauty, Amal, baby? Who will come out on top? Will this body find happiness in the arms of a man? I'd fall in love with me if I were a man! Oh, with you, lovely Amal. You are my love, my life, and my hope. Amal, I love you. I adore you, and I will let no one take you away from me. Amal, you are mine and mine alone. My name is Amal.

Despite not drinking alcohol, she was intoxicated enough to love herself. The boy she had carried during her life in her parents' house did not abandon her, even though she vehemently rejected him all the time, despite the fact she enjoyed wearing his personality occasionally between her first life and now, when the boy inside her suddenly appeared? He fell in love with a sensual, physical, instinctive girl who began to return and incarnated in stages, as if she were a phoenix rising from the ashes. Amal loves Amal.

She divided herself and overlapped her psychological, physical, hormonal, and nervous complications, shortcomings and disorders, so, in an instant, looking in the mirror with a raging masculine eye, she became her gorgeous female body, screaming, exploding with femininity.

Amal was lost for a while. She couldn't control her emotions or instincts any longer. She might have lost her mind. Her entity erupts, fragments, and nearly vanishes. She spends her days naked in bed in front of the mirror. She doesn't eat; she doesn't drink; she doesn't even leave her room. Her heaven and hell are here together.

***

Maggie, a grumpy woman with thick features and a large body, crosses the corridor looking for room 14. She reaches for the latch, inserts a key, opens the door, and enters with her shoulder as she cannot enter otherwise, since the width of her body exceeds the width of the door. She scans the room quickly and fixes her gaze on the bed. Between the bedding and quilt is a wheat-skinned body of a young woman, completely naked. She also notices that the cabinet door is open. Hajma is about to leave – she can always clean and tidy another room and come back to number 14 once the young lady has woken up and left – when she takes one last glance at the beauty, sleeping still, even though it is past noon, and something strange catches her eye. She moves closer to the sleeping lady; she's not breathing!

The hulking woman screams and runs like an elephant fleeing a predator, with lightness, speed, and fear.

A man and a woman exited the ambulance called by the hotel employee and rushed to room No. 14, led by the grumpy woman, Hajma. After a few minutes of examination, they decided to transport the young lady to the hospital as soon as possible because she was unconscious and close to a coma. She required intensive care. She had lost consciousness and hadn't eaten or drunk anything in a long time. They put plastic plugs in her mouth and pushed fluids into her, then carried her on a stretcher with an oxygen machine covering her nose.

Amal is struggling to return to normal. She woke up in a hospital, believing she was still engulfed in hallucinations that controlled her before falling into a long coma, with no one around. She sank back into a state of unconsciousness. A nurse arrived and attempted to help her regain consciousness. She brought a large lump of sterile cotton and dipped it in a quick-drying liquid, possibly cologne or something similar. Then she pressed her palm against Amal's nose. Amal trembled and it took a few moments for her to get a sense of what was going on around her.

"Who are you? Where am I?"

She said it in Arabic, in her Cairo accent.

The nurse reacted with confusion. She thought the patient was possessed and now she was speaking in tongues!

Amal realized she was in a hospital and that the woman caring for her was a nurse. She regained her breath and most of her consciousness and then spoke to her:

"Sorry. I spoke to you in my native language. I'm Egyptian. What happened to me? Why am I here?"

She said this in confused English, so the nurse's face was filled with joy and contentment as the patient improved, woke up, and began speaking English.

"Thank God you have started to recover. We were very worried about you after your state of unconsciousness deteriorated into a semi-coma. Why did you go so long without eating or drinking? Is it a case of culture shock? Are you fed up with London? The hotel clerk informed me that you are new to London. And just got here a few days ago. The most important thing right now is that you're okay."

Amal replied, thanking the nurse, but she had no idea what had happened to her. She told her that all she remembered was that she was relaxing in bed in her room.

"You were entirely naked."

"I like being naked when I'm alone!"

"The attending physician has decided you should stay with us for at least two days, until we are confident that you are in perfect health. He'll be by in an hour or so, and he'll inform you of his decision personally. How about a delicious meal?"

Amal agreed with a nod.

***

To her surprise, while thinking about what had happened to her and how she hadn't yet visited Big Ben, she had a visit from another patient. There was a knock at the door, then Harriet appeared.

"I asked after you when you were late in responding to our inquiry about our apartment room, and I was told that you were there in the hospital. What happened? Amal, get better soon!"

Amal was overjoyed. Harriet embraced her as she spread her arms out in bed.

Everything was fine with the world, she said to herself, and tears welled up in her eyes.

The conversation between them lasted a long time and was interrupted by the arrival of the doctor, who examined Amal and declared that she should stay for a day or two and that he was generally pleased with her improvement.

When Harriet was about to leave, she handed Amal a large bag she had brought with her and said, "This is for you, from Harry, Tony, and me."

The doctor advised her to stay in bed unless absolutely necessary, but she could not find out what the bag contained from the bed.

She thought, "Maybe it's better for me to be in an English family right now, and Harry and Harriet are such unusual people. How fortunate I am!"

She informed Harriet that she was moving to live with her. Harriet was delighted when she learned of the decision. She said that she was in need of good company in her home to relieve the stress of a long working day, and assured her that this would be the beginning of a successful life in London.

Of course, she told her why Harry had not come along with her. He was in the shop with Tony!

Before leaving the hospital, Amal was surprised by a strange woman visiting her!

"How are you doing these days? You don't know who I am. My name is Maggie. Simplicity Hotel is where I work. When I arrived to clean your room, number 14, I discovered you in a difficult situation. How are you doing now? They told me that you've made significant progress. You are lovely, and you should look after your health, my dear."

The strangest thing about it, in Amal's opinion, is that this enormous woman is like an elephant, with only grim expressions on her face.

Although they had never met before, she brought a bouquet and gave it to her.

Harriet had left her a bouquet, as well as a box of chocolates, an assortment of fruits, and a few small triangular sandwiches!

"I want to thank you sincerely, first for saving my life and then for your tenderness. You didn't have to go to all this trouble and expense."

"Thank the circumstances that brought me there at the right time. My love, we all need each other. And maybe you can't imagine, but I couldn't sleep after I arrived in the ambulance with you. I inquired about you every day, and I was able to come today because it was my day off.

"Now I'll leave you to rest and see you at the hotel."

***

Amal spent her hospital stay reminiscing about her brief observations of London. Fog all day and night, order, and cleanliness. The cleaners returned to work, and the government, as Harry had predicted, responded to their demands. Central heating everywhere, lighting throughout the day and night, immediate ambulance, and a hospital more luxurious than a hotel, excellent care even though I am a foreigner from Egypt. I'm not employed here, and I don't pay taxes.

Amal noticed that Maggie's bouquet of roses carried a card wishing her a speedy recovery, and that it was of a lower quality than Harriet's. She marvelled: This maid cleans hotel rooms and buys roses for someone she doesn't know!

Is this Heaven? Is this a dream? Is all of this in my head?

***

She had to spend several days in the hotel before she could move to Harry and Harriet's home. During this time, Amal, with the help of Tony, who reacted quickly to the couple's desire to assist her, opened an account in the bank and visited the National Bank of Egypt branch in London, where she withdrew some money. She keeps all her money in the bank's main office in Cairo. She buys some clothes and supplies. She doesn't forget to buy a phone and order a computer, with a request that it be bilingual in Arabic and English.

And Tony was nice, although he remained almost silent the entire time, he did not ask personal questions or speak about himself, instead explaining some of what Amal should know about the places he visited and the procedures. Because it was a long way between each location, he recommended taking the train. Amal considers riding the underground to be one of the most significant experiences to be had in this country.

She even requested a weekly train ticket and a map of the train network to study later, but after a while she became tired and bored of this silent young man most of the time, so she suggested he choose a restaurant where they could have lunch together.

But he apologized for declining the invitation because it was nearly time for his shift in the shop and he needed to return quickly. He assured her that she would find Harriet there and that she had prepared lunch.

That's exactly what happened.

"Have you seen Big Ben?" Harriet inquired.

"Unfortunately, no, we were on a practical mission, not a tourist one," she replied sadly.

"Don't worry, when you join our little family, I promise we'll do all the touristy things together. There are lots of places here I want to visit too, and Harry promised to give me a month's leave from work here; imagine an entire month, Amal!

"I didn't take any time off during my marriage, and before that, when I started working here, I took holidays, but I always preferred to go and see my family in Scotland rather than seeing the sights in London."

This time for lunch, Amal tried a new dish: fish and chips. Harriet told her it was the national dish of

the United Kingdom: a big fried fish surrounded by
a small mountain of potato chips, a bunch of boiled
green peas, a big yellow lemon cut in half, and a bit of
mayonnaise.

Amal was delighted by this delicious meal, and she
was telling Harriet and Harry, who had left the shop to
Tony and had come to lunch, about her adventures in
the underground, elevators, escalators, and descending
into the depths of these tunnels.

"But doesn't Egypt have trains?" Harry asked
her in awe.

"Of course, we have metro trains, but they don't go
as deep as your incredible trains."

"When will you decide to leave the hotel and come
live with us here?"

Amal responded to Harriet's eager question.

"The day after tomorrow."

Harriet rejoiced, but Amal did not understand
what was causing this passion and then this joy!

The young Scottish wife is looking forward to
this young Egyptian's company because she lacks the
sense of vitality, aspiration, and desire for knowledge
that she admires in Amal's character, and she wants to
go on tourist visits with her so that she, the daughter
of this country, can find out what she doesn't know
about London.

Another hidden reason is that she did not declare
it to anyone, and she does not intend to disclose it,
because there are risks that may destroy her life in
and outside of marriage. All her life. She cannot reveal
to anyone what is going on between her and Tony.
If Harry knew the secret, everything would be over:

151

marriage, business, and Tony, of course.

Everyone has skeletons in their closet!

She is eager to conceal and cover up this history, so how can she reveal to anyone at all what is going on between her and Tony?! She did not expect to find herself in this troubled relationship. He got very close to her, surrounded her whenever opportunities presented themselves, declared his love and respect for her, and expressed to her his longing, not for a casual relationship but for engagement and marriage!

He senses her suffering as the young wife of a man close to her father's age. She resisted his insistence and besieging, but her need to satisfy her pent-up desire in the arms of a young man a little older than her age and who felt the same feelings as her, made her weaken, slacken, collapse completely, surrender to him, respond to him, with repeated pursuit and insistence to the point of sympathy and begging.

***

Amal was meeting with the professor who was supervising her studies at the university, and she perceived right away that he was a tough person, very serious, his head burning with grey and ideas, speaking as if he was being inspired!

Yet he was nice, and he enjoyed all the characteristics of a gentleman. His rigour and seriousness did not put her at ease. She asked him some of the usual questions of those who came from abroad to study here, and she received the answers. She asked about the possibility of obtaining permanent residence in Britain to continue studying, and she received the answer: "No. However, you can do so if you start working after studying and get a work permit."

"Is it simple?"

"No, but it's possible."

Amal realized that continuing her studies was her stepping stone to getting temporary residency, which could take years.

She told herself that those years would give her enough time to set up her life, so she decided to leave herself alone and commit herself only to studying and working hard.

***

Amal never expected all of this to happen in such a short period, moving from Simplicity to her own room in Harry and Harriet's apartment, taking regular classes and having times that allow her to take tours around London with company. She and Harriet visit Big Ben and sometimes it is necessary to help at the shop.

With the passage of time, she became acquainted with the details of the lives of the people in this country and adapted to some of their natures and traits while despising, rejecting, or denouncing others. For example, she does not understand why people here spend so much time in pubs; the name is an abbreviation of the description of these places, it's a sort of bar, called a Public House. They are sometimes called Free Houses.

Amal noted that these places are not only for drinking alcohol; they also serve other drinks such as coffee, tea, and juices, they are restaurants that serve cold and hot meals, and they are also places where friends gather for entertainment and to play games such as pool and eat together, and some of these pubs have rooms like hotels, and because they are open to everyone, men and women, they become social centres where people meet.

Harry used to spend time in the pub near the store, drinking his favourite drink, dark beer, Guinness. He claims it helps him forget his worries and gives him the feeling that the entire world is at his command!

Amal and Harriet were sitting in the shop when Harry left them for the pub, and Tony was off at the wholesaler buying goods for the shop. They chatted and assisted customers as usual, as they were busy thinking about the next trip they would take together as part of their plan to explore the sights of London. Harriet suggested going to the British Museum, and to entice Amal, she said it was full of ancient Egyptian artefacts. Amal laughed as she revealed to Harriet that she had never visited the Egyptian Museum in Cairo!

"That's absurd; people travel to Egypt from all over the world to see the antiquities and the museum!"

"When you live in Egypt and see antiquities everywhere, it's difficult to find the motivation to visit the museum. We also have the misconception as Egyptians that the museum was built for foreign tourists, visitors, and researchers. My initial idea of the Archaeology Museum was that it was full of mummies, preserved corpses, and I'm afraid of the dead."

Their conversation was cut short when a man rushed into the store, which would have made them nervous if Harriet hadn't recognized him and reassured Amal.

The man was glum, his features dominated by expressions of confusion and shock, and he exclaimed:

"Harry!"

Harriet quickly responded, "He's in the pub."

"I know, but."

"But what?"

"I'm not sure. Come with me. We called him an ambulance."

Harriet left, dragging Amal with her and hurriedly closed the shop. She ran to the pub, with Amal running behind her.

Harry was panting and almost unable to breathe when the ambulance arrived, taking him to the hospital with Harriet. Amal had to stay and await Tony's return with the new goods.

She and Tony put the goods away and dealt with customers for half an hour, but they were tense and worried about Harry.

Their trepidation was short-lived, as Harriet called in tears to tell them her husband had died.

Despite Tony's obvious affection, Amal noticed a distinct expression on his face, but she didn't understand it; this man uttered so few words and had vague expressions as well!

★★★

Tony was living in the apartment a year after Harry died, and he took the place of Harriet's husband. Although they did not register their marriage, did not have a wedding, and did not go to church or the civil registry!

These facts astounded Amal, but she soon realized that this is a common social situation in this country, that it is not illegal and is accepted by society as based on consent between men and women.

Amal was busy with her studies, and a new young man was hired to work in the shop. Tony brought him to the shop and Amal got to know him. His name was Derek, and he was kind, active, and talkative. He asked her about her studies and future plans, and whether she would continue to live there after studying or whether she would return to Egypt. He laughed cheerfully, saying, "Why don't you take me to visit your wonderful country? Why don't we drop everything and fly to Egypt?"

Amal laughed as she looked at this young Englishman who was fond of Egypt—as he told her when they met for the first time—starting to look at him with a woman's eye and admiring him, and she found herself starting long conversations with him and accepting his invitation to meet in the pub, where he reveals his personality and she learns more about his future aspirations.

She asked him, "Do your words mean you won't be working in the shop for long?"

"Of course, this is a stage that I will move past when I have the ability to move on to the next step."

"What's the next step?"

"I'm not sure, but what I really want is to resume my university studies, which were cut short because of circumstances beyond my control, perhaps enrol in a night class, study history, and possibly specialize in Egyptology. Who knows!?"

★★★

Amal is sitting alone in her room; she enjoys sitting alone to meditate, review her lessons, or browse the Internet, but she is now preoccupied with an idea that has taken over her mind and her entire being: Will I have a future with Derek?!

She had begun to feel some time ago that having a man in her life had become a necessity, perhaps because she has now lived together with Harriet and Tony in the next room. Before that, nothing attracting her attention had happened in the same room. Amal knows she's still young for all of this, but why not?

She recalls a long chain of memories about her mother and her scandalous story with her father, Adawi, and how, as a teenager, she surrendered to her sensual desires and was tempted by the pleasure of having sex with him, so the present and the future were lost to her.

The tape of memories goes through a quick succession of snapshots of situations and run-ins that Amal had had with the boys at school, as well as the fleeting moments when she was tempted by the beginnings of her sense of femininity, despite the harshness of those who messed with her, and the story of a man who only asked her to let him see her body naked! The strange man who would have raped her had she not been—as he desired—a boy! And a glimpse from what had happened to her with the lesbian, Inshirah.

The chain of memories is severed by the sounds of Harriet's groans in the next room during her tumultuous intimacy with Tony. Now Harriet has a voice in bed. She gave in to the idea of safety in Harry's house and forgot she was a woman. Now I have found an explanation for the mysterious behaviour between her and Tony while Harry was alive. I felt their closeness, which I thought was a kin relationship. I hadn't thought about it properly, a female whose femininity was out of order with Harry and with a man like Tony hovering around. Had she succumbed to her instincts and his youth while her husband was alive?

Was the husband aware of what they were up to?

Questions without answers. Amal's mind was exhausted, and she rose naked from her bed to face herself in front of the cupboard mirror in her small room, contemplating the features of her young body, reminding herself that she was filling this body with science and knowledge until it was complete, recalling Derek's comment about his desire to complete his university education. Oh Derek. Will I have a future with this young man who only talk about the future?

***

Harriet was preoccupied with the changes in her life and Tony's initiative to modernize the shop, and most importantly, Amal noticed apparent changes in her; she went through a renewal too!

She now cares about her overall appearance, buys chic clothes, and attends to every detail of her femininity. Apparently, her relationship with Tony has restored her sense of self and renewed her youth.

All of this did not stop Harriet from joining Amal in some conversations and picnics. They went to Hyde Park together, and Amal was astonished that it was a large open park in the heart of London, unlike any park in Cairo. However, it was the first time either of them had been there, but she noticed that Harriet was not equally surprised.

Talking to her, she learned from her that large gardens existed in many places throughout this country, not just the capital. She knew of several in Scotland, where she grew up.

She told her about some of these gardens, but Amal was left wondering, "By the way, why did you leave your country and travel to the capital?"

She remained silent for a moment, as if organizing her thoughts, before saying, "Ah, this is a long story, Amal. What made you think about that now?"

"I didn't mean to bother you, love, let's change the subject."

"No. No. You have now entered my life and live with me at home, and I love you, and I will not hide the matter from you. I ran away from my family because there was a dispute between me and my father and my brothers, and there was no solution other than to leave the village in search of a better life. I hated being just the farmer's daughter, a peasant, in a world full of aspirations and developments that I heard about and watched on TV and at the cinema. If I had stayed there, I would have committed suicide.

"True, my ambitions are limited, but I despised caring for pigs, preparing food, baking bread, and the like, and I refused to be a carbon copy of my mother.

"Although I had not completed my education, I was never eager to enter university; I wanted to break free from this evil circle."

She said this while clenching her teeth.

We were sitting on the shore of a lake in the middle of the vast Hyde Park, watching a paddle of ducks swim happily and calmly.

Harriet wished she could swim like one of these ducks, calmly, freely, and happily.

But then Amal had a thought: "Do you think what you wished for yourself has come true?"

"Not entirely, but I am better off. Even though my disagreement with my family did not last long, and years before my father died, he had understood, come to terms with, and accepted my point of view, albeit reluctantly."

Amal was thinking of her past life and her suffering, and it occurred to her that she, too, should tell some of her story, but for some inexplicable reason, she immediately retracted.

Harriet continued, "I started out working in the shop and living in the apartment, but now I am its owner and owner of the apartment, and I live with a suitable person with whom I share everything, and we are striving to develop the business so that we can spend more time together."

Amal interrupted her. "But, dear Harriet, let me ask you: did your relationship with Tony begin while Harry was alive?"

Amal retreated after noticing signs of annoyance at this open confrontation on Harriet's face. "I'm sorry, you don't have to answer my question, which I think was a slip of the tongue; please forgive me; I withdraw the question."

Harriet burst out laughing and said, "What's with your regret and apology, crazy woman? You and I are as close as two sisters, and I have the right to answer for our relationship to grow stronger. Ask me whatever you want; there are no barriers or secrets between us. This is how I feel about you, and I believe it is the same way you feel about me, and that's how I took your question."

Amal was surprised and felt that the next step was to tell her story, but before she could catch her breath and begin, Harriet had answered her question. "You know, Amal, that I was 25 years younger than Harry, and that we married after his late wife died suddenly, and that he took pity on me, and I took pity on him. After this shock, he could have looked for a suitable wife and kept me as his assistant in the shop, but he didn't. I could have refused to associate with him, but I agreed. We don't create circumstances, Amal, we just deal with them. At that time, I was afraid of the future. I said, 'a new wife will come'. I don't know what her position will be towards me and my living in the apartment. What if we don't understand each other and she asks for me to be fired from my job? I was afraid of this and other things because I am a stranger here and I didn't want to go back to my family in the far north, as a misguided, failed, miserable daughter. Do you understand my circumstances?

"As for Tony, my husband Harry brought him on, and he might have been aware of what was going on between us in secret, as he occasionally gave signs that suggested he knew what was going on. Or maybe not, I'm not sure. Although he strictly resolved not to give Tony the room you live in now, which is the room where I lived while his wife was alive. It was his wife who brought me to work in the shop. Do you know why he did that? So, he wasn't forced to recognise what was going on between Tony and me!

"As for Tony himself, I believe he sensed my predicament and my suffering as a woman, and perhaps sensed that Harry knew what was going on and he perhaps deliberately suggested to us that he didn't know, perhaps to save face, perhaps because he felt sorry for me.

"Tony was always urging me to live my life as a woman with him, not stealing me from my husband, and he always promised to marry me one day."

Amal, faced with this incredible amount of frankness from a woman, couldn't contain herself, and she sat with her mouth wide open, excited, and shocked by what she was hearing, thinking to herself, these are extraordinary people.

Amal tried to regain her equilibrium, and asked Harriet, "But you're not married, are you?"

Harriet laughed. "There's a secret behind that. You might not think it, but I get a special monthly pension as a widow, and if I get married, I won't be entitled to that amount, and Tony and I are planning to expand our business, so we'll need that pension."

After the outing to Hyde Park, their friendship became stronger and deeper. Amal was increasingly reassuring to Harriet, despite her behaviour, which was still a source of contention between Amal and her, and the stories of this young wife triggered her feelings of burning desire for an intimate relationship.

***

At the university, the professor supervising her grant asked her to submit a brief report on an English writer she believed had impacted on a genre of English and world literature; he accompanied her to the library to introduce her to the librarians who would assist her in borrowing books and reference materials; and he explained that the results would determine if she should be allowed to continue her studies.

This request hit her like a ton of bricks; it was a matter of life and death for her; she could either realize her dream of staying here or face the nightmare of ending everything and returning disappointed to where she came from.

She has three months, no less or more; she has been in London for more than a year, and her supervisor's overall impression is 'good', 'improving', and 'promising', as he put it, which prompted him to extend the grant period; but the time has come for hard work, immersion in research, studying, reviewing books and references, and training in good research practices and proficiency, formulating and sequencing in correct, cohesive, expressive academic language.

The professor did not neglect to remind her of the importance of looking at similar studies and research in the library's archives, provided she not fall into the trap of imitating or copying what she reads, or even repeating ideas and meanings; a study containing a new, innovative point of view, no matter how strange, was what was required.

Will I be able to accomplish all of this?

Amal questioned herself, but received no clear answer; however, her desire to remain here was her strongest motivator. A matter of life or death, she said to herself.

The computer helped a lot, as did the library visits. She stopped doing anything except research and studying, and she forgot about her need for a relationship with a man. She was able to reach the ability of mastery and innovation because she intensified her attention and exerted all her energy, sharpening all her ideas and insisting on achieving the highest level of performance.

This is what the supervising professor told her after reviewing her research.

After much deliberation, she chose Mary Shelley as a topic for her research because, among dozens of prominent names in the history of English literature, Mary Shelley is a woman, and the emergence of women and their prominence in the world of literature in Britain is rare, or very limited – it wouldn't take you long to list all the names. Amal thought to herself that this writer was different from the rest of the female writers because she has invented something new in all world literature, not just English. This genre is now called Science Fiction. This innovation alone is enough to set Mary Shelley apart. There is also an important reason to highlight the importance of this writer – as Amal sees it – which is that she was subjected to a harsh campaign from critics, all of whom were men, claiming that her novel Frankenstein was not written by her and its real author was actually her husband, the eminent poet Percy Shelley.

Amal was interested in going above and beyond to refute this accusation by analysing the lexical dictionary composed by Mary's famous poet husband, Mary Shelley's dictionary, and her vocabulary in the novel. Amal felt that she was not only writing a paper that would guarantee her survival in this country, but also advocating for her cause as a woman, as Mary Shelley's works and writings spread awareness about women's rights.

While Amal waited for the supervisor's opinion, she had a vague feeling that he would find one or more flaws in the text, or a weakness in extracting an unprecedented critical idea, but when he spoke, she felt hope.

The supervisor proposed to the university committee that the research be reviewed and considered for a master's thesis, and his proposal was accepted, and the research was deemed appropriate for a master's degree.

When the decision was made to extend her period of scholarship to get the PHD degree, she saw this as a new beginning for her and threw a small party, inviting her supervising professor and two classmates she had met at university, as well as Harriet, Tony, and the new young man in the shop, Derek, the university librarian, and Peter.

Does her academic success mean she will specialise in English literature?

She was asking herself this during her long sessions with herself, and after contemplation and reflection, she discovered that her answer to the question was no. She knows that her desire to stay in London was her true motivation, and she knows that she has no real inclinations in that direction. The issue is just an ordinary study, arduous and tiring, but she passed successfully.

This means, Amal, she thinks to herself, that you have other interests. What are they?

She plunged into deep thought, in search of an answer, but got nowhere. Do you want to qualify for a specific job? Do you want to live as a female, without work, until a lover stumbles across you or you find one and the matter develops into marriage and he becomes your husband?

Her sense of financial security and lack of need for money frequently control her thinking about the future; she is not busy earning a living, and she does not look forward – at least for the foreseeable future – to preparing herself for a specific profession, and even discussing a doctorate does not represent an exciting incentive for her. This is not my goal.

So, Amal, what is your goal?

She asks herself and waits for an answer, but no answer comes.

Confusion is my life. At every stage, I am in a state of confusion, and this curse adds to the stress of being alone. I have no one around me to turn to. No one. The supervising doctor will not help me and advise me because this is not his business, and he will surely tell me that this is a personal matter that no one is allowed to interfere in, and none of the residents of the house, Harriet and Tony, are fit to give me advice on this matter, no one here fills the same role as Haja Kamela or Hajj Shehata. I do not think Derek is fit to advise me, and it is the same case with Peter.

Ah. Peter. I had forgotten about him for a while, and I remembered him thinking of the names of the people I wanted to invite to the party, and to my surprise, he came, although he had left Simplicity Hotel some time ago and was on a business assignment in the Lake District, but he promised me he would come, and he came. We talked, and he told me about the developments in his work, and that he was in Tokyo with a group of models to advertise for some fashion houses and he told me he would return to London because he has several tasks to do for his job. I was surprised when he asked me: "What is the long-term benefit of all this academic activity? Do you want to become a doctor of English literature? How much will this earn you? Nothing compared to the income of any successful and distinguished model. I don't know what you see for yourself in the future, and I don't think you know right now!"

The strange thing is that this Peter, whom I only knew for a short time before he became preoccupied with his work and travels, believes I am trapped in a whirlpool and can't define my future goals!

Is this how exposed I am? What would he think of me if he knew what I haven't told anyone, any one at all!?

I said to myself: "If you, a decent girl, discovered your ability to immerse yourself in English literature and write a decent and unique study in it—as the members of the committee had said about me – what's preventing you from continuing the matter is that you discovered within yourself an interest that would not have occurred to you if it had not been for the challenges you faced?"

I decided to look forward and think about Amal. After several years, I could become a doctor and professor of English literature. Will I work here at a British university, or in an Egyptian or Arab university?

As Peter asked, is that what I'm looking for, and do I see myself in this field?

To be honest, I don't think I can immerse myself in this field. I need work that makes me feel my femininity, which I missed during the years I was deprived of it, my formative years, and English literature will not do that for me. What if I work in a profession like the one Peter told me about? I accompanied him on a business trip, and I watched and witnessed how things were when we went to Richmond Park. Femininity is manifest there. I feel more of myself, and a more important feature is that working as a model will give me a rare opportunity to roam around the world, and as I understood from the models that it is not as easy a job as it seems from the surface, as there are hardships, including intense and continuous care of the body, health and beauty, and among them the frequent travel and trips, and competition. There is another thing a model told me during our trip to Richmond Park, which is related to the model's age, which is a short career. Within a few years, she will find herself getting older and entering the stage of wrinkles and aging, and then she will not find anyone looking for her from fashion or publicity agencies.

I was in my room, and I stood naked in front of the large mirror, contemplating it, staring in the mirror, and searching with my eyes for my own features— Peter told me I had very special qualities in terms of complexion, freshness, softness, and aesthetics in the anatomy of the face, and the general figure of this charming eastern body.

And don't forget, Amal, I tell myself, the lights, fame, plenty of money, and entry into high-end societies from the top will compensate you for the years of torment, reviving your sense of femininity and beauty, and providing you with enough to save for old age.

I mulled over the idea in my head, considering the dangers and risks, but I found myself motivated to do it.

The Beginning

BV - #0015 - 081222 - C0 - 203/127/10 - PB - 9781915338747 - Matt Lamination